PENGUIN CLASSICS

CYRANO DE BERGERAC

Born in Marseille in 1868, EDMOND ROSTAND came to Paris as a student in 1884 and quickly began to move in literary circles. Before he was twenty he had won the annual prize of the Académie de Marseille for an essay on the topic 'Two Provençal novelists', which drew the unlikely comparison between Honoré d'Urfé, the seventeenth-century writer of pastoral romance, and Émile Zola, the then notorious chronicler of contemporary low life. Married at twenty-two and a father at twenty-three, Rostand had his first play performed at the Comédie-Française when he was twenty-six and by the following year was writing vehicles for Sarah Bernhardt and other notable actors of the time. *Cyrano de Bergerac* (1897) was an enormous success which won him immediate election to the Légion d'Honneur and two years later to the Académie Française. Rostand seems, however, to have been unhappy with the fame and public curiosity the play attracted to his family; from 1900 he suffered increasingly from lung and nervous troubles and lived more and more on the country estate he had bought in the Pyrenees. He wrote two further plays, *L'Aiglon* (1900), in which the then fifty-five-year-old Sarah Bernhardt played the twenty-year-old son of Napoleon I, to great acclaim, and in 1910 the long-promised *Chantecler*, in which the main characters are birds and were again played – in beaks and feathers – by some of the most famous actors of the day. Though both of these plays were successful, neither was a hit on the scale of *Cyrano*.

Judged medically unfit to serve in the First World War, Rostand died aged fifty in the world influenza pandemic of 1918.

CAROL CLARK is an Emeritus Fellow of Balliol College, Oxford. She taught French there for many years, lecturing particularly on seventeenth- and nineteenth-century topics. She has previously translated Baudelaire and Proust for Penguin.

T0021410

EDMOND ROSTAND

Cyrano de Bergerac

Translated with an Introduction and Notes by
CAROL CLARK

PENGUIN BOOKS

PENGUIN CLASSICS

Published by the Penguin Group
Penguin Books Ltd, 80 Strand, London WC2R 0RL, England
Penguin Group (USA) Inc., 375 Hudson Street, New York, New York 10014, USA
Penguin Group (Canada), 90 Eglinton Avenue East, Suite 700, Toronto, Ontario, Canada M4P 2Y3
(a division of Pearson Penguin Canada Inc.)
Penguin Ireland, 25 St Stephen's Green, Dublin 2, Ireland
(a division of Penguin Books Ltd)
Penguin Group (Australia), 250 Camberwell Road, Camberwell, Victoria 3124, Australia
(a division of Pearson Australia Group Pty Ltd)
Penguin Books India Pvt Ltd, 11, Community Centre, Panchsheel Park, New Delhi – 110 017, India
Penguin Books (NZ), cnr Airborne and Rosedale Roads, Albany, Auckland 1310, New Zealand
(a division of Pearson New Zealand Ltd)
Penguin Books (South Africa) (Pty) Ltd, 24 Sturdee Avenue, Rosebank, Johannesburg 2196, South Africa

Penguin Books Ltd, Registered Offices: 80 Strand, London WC2R 0RL, England

www.penguin.com

Published in Penguin Classics 2006

029

This edition and translation copyright © Carol Clark, 2005
All rights reserved

The moral right of the translator has been asserted

Set in 10.25/12.25 pt PostScript Adobe Sabon
Typeset by Rowland Phototypesetting Ltd, Bury St Edmunds, Suffolk
Printed and bound in Great Britain by Clays Ltd, Elcograf S.p.A.

ISBN-13: 978-0-140-44968-6

www.greenpenguin.co.uk

MIX
Paper from
responsible sources
FSC
www.fsc.org
FSC™ C018179

Penguin Books is committed to a sustainable
future for our business, our readers and our planet.
This book is made from Forest Stewardship
Council™ certified paper.

Contents

Chronology

1868 Edmond Rostand born in Marseille.

1878–84 Attends the Lycée de Marseille.

1884 Moves to Paris to attend the Collège Stanislas.

1887 Wins the annual prize of the Académie de Marseille for an essay on *Two Provençal Novelists: Honoré d'Urfé and Émile Zola* (an extremely unlikely pairing).

1888 Nominally a law student in Paris, begins to write for the theatre.

1890 Marries Rosemonde Gérard; publishes first collection of verse, *Les Musardises* (Daydreaming).

1894 His play *Les Romanesques* (Romantic Characters) is put on at the Comédie-Française (most unusual for such a young writer) and well received.

Offers his next play, *La Princesse lointaine* (The Faraway Princess), to Sarah Bernhardt, the greatest actress of the day: she accepts.

1895 A strongly cast and lavish production of *La Princesse lointaine* at the Théâtre de la Renaissance is only a moderate success.

1896 During the Dreyfus case, takes the side of the unjustly accused Captain Dreyfus.

1897 April: *La Samaritaine* (The Woman of Samaria), written for Sarah Bernhardt, is well received.

December: *Cyrano de Bergerac* is a huge success.

1898 1 January: Made a Chevalier of the Légion d'Honneur in the New Year list.

6 January: As his official New Year's visit to the theatre,

the President of France, Félix Faure, takes his family to see *Cyrano*.

1900 *L'Aiglon* (The Young Eagle), with Sarah Bernhardt, is a success, but not comparable to *Cyrano*. Rostand begins to suffer from lung and nerve troubles.

1901 Buys a villa at Cambo, in the South of France, and begins to spend more and more of his time there.

    May: elected to the Académie Française (See I, ii, n. 1).

1908 December: *Chantecler* (Chanticleer), promised to Constant Coquelin for four years, is finally delivered.

1909 January: Coquelin dies. Lucien Guitry takes over the part of Chanticleer.

1910 The long-awaited *Chantecler* opens at the Porte Saint-Martin, to only moderate notices.

1913 Premiere of Walter Damrosch's opera *Cyrano de Bergerac* at the Metropolitan Opera, New York.

    Revival of *Cyrano* at the Porte Saint-Martin and celebration of its thousandth performance there.

1914 Rostand's poor health prevents him from volunteering in the First World War.

1916 Begins to take an interest in the cinema, writing to a friend that 'Le "ciné" a un avenir énorme' (The 'movies', as they say, have an enormous future). Publishes patriotic poems.

1918 Days after the armistice, succumbs to the world-wide epidemic of Spanish flu. Dies, aged fifty.

Introduction

Cyrano de Bergerac was one of the great theatrical successes of the nineteenth century, if not of all time. Edmond Rostand devised it as a vehicle for the highly popular actor Constant Coquelin (then aged fifty-six) and in December 1897 it was produced regardless of expense at the thousand-seat Théâtre de la Porte Saint-Martin in Paris, where it was an immediate sell-out and ran for nearly three years. It was staged in New York, in French, in October 1898, again to great acclaim, and three different American publishers had the French text in print by the next year, soon to be followed by several different translations. Since then it has been constantly revived, in French, English and many other languages, staged several times as an opera and repeatedly filmed. Jean-Paul Rappeneau's film of 1990, with Gérard Depardieu in the title role, brought the story to a whole new audience in France, Britain and the United States.

The play originally held, and to an extent still holds, a particular appeal for French audiences, but its worldwide and continuing success must be based on more general factors. It is a story of four loves (Christian's for Roxane and hers for him, Cyrano's for Roxane and, finally, hers for Cyrano), none of which, due to a series of dramatic ironies, is ever consummated except in death. This is romantic enough, but there is also a wry realism in the play which is based on universal human insecurities, on our belief that we cannot be loved because the qualities that win love are found only in others: the clever man believes he is too ugly, the handsome man that he is too stupid. In commonplace characters such feelings might breed only resentment, and Rostand's villain, De Guiche, responds to Cyrano's superior wit and Christian's youthful radiance with a dastardly scheme of revenge. But the two male leads behave nobly. Their rivalry is subsumed in friendship, and each sacrifices himself, or tries to sacrifice himself, for the other: Cyrano in Act III, Christian in Act IV, scene ix, and Cyrano again, most quixotically, after Christian's death.

This combination of noble characters, stirring events and romantic love themes was characteristic of the nineteenth-century popular theatre: Rostand added a much less common element of humour (an ugly, self-mocking hero!), and a dizzy linguistic ingenuity which was truly original (see A Note on the Translation). But *Cyrano* acquired a new and unintended resonance twenty years later with the events of the First World War.

Critics have argued that even in 1897 the play, with its stress on the theme of '*panache*' and its Act IV scenes of resistance against overwhelming odds, appealed to French pride, still wounded after their rapid defeat in the Franco-Prussian war of 1870. But seventeen years after the creation of *Cyrano* France was at war with Germany again, putting up a desperate and this time more successful resistance on the very same territory on which Rostand's cadets must fight in Act IV of our play, and which the Prussians had overrun in the earlier defeat. This new war was eventually to take the lives of a million Frenchmen, and many young men must have found themselves in the situation of Cyrano, returning alive to face the young fiancée of a dead friend and feeling a superstitious reverence for a love sealed in blood. The play thus acquired a dreadful topicality, and, though intellectual critics were dismissive of it in the 1920s, *Cyrano* may have served to fuel the French spirit of resistance in both World Wars. Willy de Spens, in his introduction to the 1989 Garnier-Flammarion edition of *Cyrano*, recalls hearing, in his youth, an elderly general describe it as 'the play that won us the war'.

On a slightly lighter note, a new element of the French fightback in the First World War was an official scheme to encourage young women, even of the upper classes, to boost the morale of the troops not only by knitting scarves or making jam but in a more personal way, by sending parcels and letters to individual soldiers previously unknown to them. (For a young lady to correspond in this way with a stranger would formerly have been regarded as shocking.) Young women who entered into this idealized relationship with young men, many of whom they must have realized were doomed to die, were known as *marraines*, godmothers, and one wonders to what extent Roxane's fairytale behaviour in Act IV may have been seen as a model and justification for the programme.

The original production of *Cyrano* had forty-three speaking parts, as well as the 'crowd, *bourgeois*, noblemen, musketeers, pickpockets, bakers, poets, cadets, actors, musicians, pages, children, soldiers, Spaniards, theatre-goers, *précieuses*, actresses, middle-class wives, nuns, etc.' who walked on in the various scenes. As well as costumes for these countless bodies, it required five solidly built and elaborately dressed sets, one for each act, which are described in detail in the printed text. Such a triumph of middlebrow spectacle could never be re-created today, unless in the cinema. Indeed, on a first reading of the play, one is tempted to think that it is simply unstageable with the kinds of resources available to a present-day director. But its dramatic power is such that much of it survives even in a seriously scaled-down staging. I saw an extremely effective and moving production in Paris in 2004 by the Théâtre du Nord-Ouest, a repertory company of about eight performing in a disused cinema with minimal scenery and props (but convincing costume).

The text, therefore, is undoubtedly a product of the theatre, and of the theatre of a particular time. Indeed, the more one reads it, the more one is struck by resemblances to other kinds of theatrical spectacle popular in the late nineteenth century, both in France and England. The setting of the play and the on-stage sword-fights recall swashbuckling historical drama, while scenes based on clever trickery (Roxane leading her middle-aged admirer up the garden path in Act III, scene ii, or Cyrano deliberately delaying him in Act III, scene xiii) could, if they were not in verse, come from the contemporary *vaudeville* (what we call French farce). There is something of the opera in the use of crowds to react to the key actions of the principal characters, and the role given to the youthful choruses with their older leaders (the cadets and Carbon, the novices and Mother Margaret). But, more oddly, the grouping of Cyrano, Roxane and the cadets in Act IV also recalls the 'alternative family' formed by Peter, Wendy and the Lost Boys in *Peter Pan* (1904), while the smooth villain De Guiche has something of Captain Hook about him. Rostand's knowing use of impossibly ingenious rhymes must also remind an English reader of Gilbert's libretti for the Savoy operas.

But though conceived for the theatre, *Cyrano de Bergerac* also appeals to the reader. First published in 1898, the text has never been out of print since, and is currently available in France in all four of the main paperback series. It is perhaps with a view to private reading, and to help the reader to visualize his play, that Rostand includes in the printed text such very full descriptions of the sets, and also what must strike the English-speaking reader as unnecessary stage directions of the 'to Christian' and 'to Roxane' sort. Acts have titles, like chapters of a novel, and the longer directions include suggestions impossible to realize on stage. For example, Rostand indicates at the beginning of Act IV that Christian, Cyrano and the cadets are notably thinner and paler than they were at the end of Act III, when in real time about ten minutes have elapsed. Such indications point to a play intended to be read as well as staged, perhaps following the example of the truly unactable *Théâtre dans un fauteuil* of Alfred de Musset (1810–57) (Armchair Theatre, but long before the television series of that name). All in all, it is not surprising that *Cyrano de Bergerac* is rarely if ever played without cuts. I have translated the whole text as faithfully as I can, and left the question of cuts to directors who may decide to stage it in future.

Though plainly rooted in the world of 1897, the play also belongs, in intention at least, to the world of 1640 (see Historical Note). It is clear that Rostand had researched the

earlier period, using some original sources. But his repre-
sentation of life under Louis XIII also owes a great deal to
nineteenth-century versions of it, notably the novels of Alexandre Dumas. The bold, anarchic life of the men in the play,
mingling bloodthirstiness with humour, corresponds very
closely to the 1897 theatre-goer's idea of seventeenth-century
manners; but that was in turn coloured by Dumas's *Three
Musketeers* (1844). Rostand's depiction of seventeenth-century
literary life, whether the world of the *précieuses* to which
Roxane belongs, or that of actors struggling with unruly audiences, or of starving poets sustained by the output of Ragueneau's *pâtisserie*, shows familiarity with writings of the time,
but the images of these various social groups do again correspond closely to nineteenth-century stereotypes of them. Rather
than documentary-style realism, Rostand offers a knowing,
allusive treatment of seventeenth-century life which flatters the
audience in its knowledge, or imagined knowledge, of the
period. In this the play resembles a modern script like Tom
Stoppard's for the film *Shakespeare in Love* (1998). The language of *Cyrano*, however, is layered in a more complex fashion
than that of any film script. Cyrano is not just a seventeenth-
century swordsman and wit, or a nineteenth-century version
of one. His extravagant passion for Roxane and his sense of
differentness, of being excluded from the life of ordinary human
beings, make him very like a Romantic hero of the earlier
nineteenth century, while his cultivated eccentricity – dining on
a grape, a glass of water and half a macaroon when he is
starving, for example (I, v, 450–53) – suggests a poet of the
later Decadent school, contemporary with the play itself. All
these different layers of the character are reflected in the rich
and highly artificial language of the text.

Whereas by 1897 the great majority of plays written for
the commercial theatre were in prose, *Cyrano* is written in
alexandrine couplets, like the seventeenth-century tragedies of
Corneille and Racine (and the Romantic *drames* of Victor
Hugo). But it does not observe any of the other rules of classical
dramatic writing, whether in the construction of the play or the
use of verse. The famous 'rule of the three unities', based on

Aristotle's *Poetics* but elaborated by the dramatic theorists of
the seventeenth century, required the whole action of a play to
be completed within twenty-four hours. Rostand, however, sets
Acts I–IV over a period of some weeks in 1640 (Act II happens
the day after Act I, but Roxane and Christian have to have had
several meetings between Acts II and III, and at the beginning
of Act IV the siege of Arras has been going on for weeks), while
Act V is set fifteen years later. (This time lapse is absolutely
essential to the play since it allows us to measure the extent of
Cyrano's devotion to Roxane. In the elegiac atmosphere of
the last act, we mentally compare the time-worn, ailing figure
Cyrano now cuts not only with the dashing swordsman of Act I
but with the shining image of Christian, preserved in eternal
youth by his death.)

All the action of a classical play must take place in a single
location, usually an all-purpose ante-room in a palace, but
Rostand changes location with each act, thus appealing to the
1897 audience's taste for elaborate stage pictures. Instead of
the sustained seriousness of classical theatre, we have a constant
alternation between passion and humour. Victor Hugo had
already taught that serious drama, in imitation (he thought) of
Shakespeare, should bring together '*le grotesque et le sublime*',
but Rostand does not really work in either of these modes:
his palette ranges between intense feeling and clever, allusive
humour employing much irony and even parody. Though he
shows great virtuosity in his use of the twelve-syllable alexandrine line, he does not hesitate to manhandle it, constantly
breaking the line, dividing it between two or more speakers in
a conversational way (where the rule had been that the line was
only broken at moments of high drama), and puncturing its
dignity by mixing it with colloquial language, deliberate anachronisms and comical rhymes. Again, though this shocked some
of the poets of the day, we can imagine it would have pleased
audiences who had sat through the staider performances of the
Comédie-Française, and no doubt had been made, in their
schooldays, to learn famous alexandrine *tirades* by heart.
(Again, one recalls the frequent parody of grand opera, alternat-
ing with moments of apparently genuine feeling, in the Gilbert

and Sullivan scores: Rostand supplies both the Gilbert and the Sullivan elements.) The element of semi-comic virtuosity in Rostand's use of the alexandrine is such an important part of the appeal of the play that I felt I must try to keep something of it in my version. English alexandrines are rarely successful, so I chose in the end a loose five-beat line suggestive (I hope) of blank verse, the metre most associated with heroic drama in English.

A Note on the Translation

Act III, scenes iv–vii, the famous balcony scene, provides an excellent introduction to the difficulties of translating this play. The formula is familiar: as well as the obvious memories of Shakespeare, there are more closely similar scenes in Molière's *Dom Juan* and Mozart's opera based on it, *Don Giovanni*. But those are cruelly farcical scenes, in which the lady is being mocked by the two men. Here the scene modulates from fairly broad comedy at the beginning (the tongue-tied Christian, scene v), through witty linguistic play (scene vii), to an increasingly passionate declaration by Cyrano under the cover of darkness. Familiar, even aggressive language between Cyrano and Christian alternates with the high-flown, over-ingenious language of seventeenth-century love poetry. Cyrano can deploy this language with the best, but from line 246 onwards he becomes increasingly impatient with it and tries to address Roxane more directly, drawing upon immediate sense-impressions. His language then comes to resemble the Symbolist poetry of 1897 rather than the *précieux* poetry of 1640, until by l. 272 it has become almost incoherent with passion (though still voiced in correctly formed alexandrines). The register of the text is therefore extremely inconsistent, and any attempt at a faithful translation must be inconsistent in the same way.

Act III, scene xiii presents a particular challenge in that Cyrano is supposed to adopt a regional accent (the 'switching' that I have rendered by the sound 'krk, krk' is in Rostand's original text as *Cric! crac!*). But what accent? In French, presumably a

Gascon one, though the only example of 'Gascon' that Rostand gives ('*jeung*' for '*jeun*' at l. 2073 of the original text) is in fact more characteristic of his native Marseille. The translator would favour using a Scottish accent at this point, for several reasons. For British readers or hearers, it is associated with bravery and stubbornness (the Scottish regiments are famous in the history and present service of the British army). Scots are traditionally underdogs, poor and proud, like Rostand's Gascons: less admirably, they are seen as heavy drinkers, and Cyrano is pretending to be drunk at this point. The buttonholing, confidential drunk is a traditional Scottish comic type, from Will Fyffe in the 1920s ('I Belong To Glasgow') to Billy Connolly today. Finally, it is my own original accent. But a director may well wish to use a different accent that his Cyrano is more familiar with (or none at all, though the plot requires it as part of Cyrano's disguise). For an American audience a Southern accent might have some suitable associations, and the story of the journey to the moon would fit well into the Southern 'tall tale' tradition. My translation includes very small hints of Scottish vernacular in Cyrano's first couple of speeches, leaving it to the discretion of the actor to continue (as Shaw does, much more broadly, with Eliza's Cockney in *Pygmalion*). A director curious to see a complete version in broad Scots should consult Edwin Morgan's translation of the play (see Further Reading). Whatever accent is chosen could probably become less marked as the content of Cyrano's speeches becomes more learned, and as De Guiche is successfully drawn in to the deception.

There is only one word in the play which is really untranslatable, and that is unfortunately the final and most important word – *panache*. Its primary meaning is a plume, particularly the plume on a helmet, and this is the only meaning given in Littré's dictionary of 1868 (the French equivalent of the original *OED*). But by the early twentieth century it had acquired in French the secondary meaning of dash or swagger: '*avoir du panache*' is rendered in the Robert dictionary of 1933 as '*avoir fière allure*' (another almost untranslatable phrase, unfortunately). The first illustrative quotation suggests that in military circles it was by then a term of praise, since it says that the *'exemple et contagion'* of an officer's *panache* could inspire his troops to feats of daring (as Cyrano's does at the end of Act IV of our play). The remaining illustrative quotations, however, taken from intellectuals like André Gide and Jean Dutourd, suggest that for them *panache* was a much more suspect value. It seems quite likely that Rostand was responsible for the establishment, or at any rate the popularizing, of *panache* in its figurative sense. Later editions of the *Robert* suggest as synonyms *éclat* (literally, brilliance; eye-catching quality), *brio* and *bravoure*. The latter two, interestingly, are borrowings from Italian: *bravoure* can mean either bravery or bravura. 'Panache' in the sense of a plume does exist in English, but is rare. For us the figurative meaning, borrowed from French, is the primary one.

Cyrano's dying words – *'mon panache'* – must refer to the actual plume on his hat, since he speaks of doffing it and sweeping the floor of heaven with it. But it also seems to refer metaphorically to some defining aspect of his character. And this quality must, I believe, be a morally admirable one, or one at any rate that his hearers (whether of 1640 or 1897) would have recognized as morally admirable: certainly something more than the definition we find in the *Concise Oxford* of 2004: 'flamboyant confidence of style or manner'. Whatever the precise meaning of *'panache'*, it is something that many French people still admire, and it is encapsulated for them by this play. The first illustrative phrase in the *Petit Robert* (the standard school dictionary) of 2004 is *'le panache de Cyrano'*. Finding an English equivalent for this totemic object, and at the same time a concluding rhyme, was, I am afraid, beyond me.

I have followed Rostand's own division of the acts into scenes. The French way of doing this, in published play texts, is to begin a new scene whenever a character enters or leaves the stage (though Rostand is rather lax in observing this rule and characters do leave the stage and sometimes return in the course of what is set out as a single scene). A change of scene does not, therefore, indicate a change of location, and should not even be marked by a pause in the dialogue unless one is specified in the text. In fact, Rostand often has a change of scene, in this sense, occurring in the middle of a line of verse, and it is important that the rhythm should be sustained across what is simply a visual break in the text.

A note on pronunciation. French words are lightly stressed on the last syllable, except where that is the so-called 'mute *e*'. But when speaking English it can sound very artificial to stress the characters' names in this way. I therefore suggest stressing them as follows:

Belle'rose
Bris'saille
Car'bon (because 'Carbon sounds even worse)
'Christian
'Cuigy
'Cyrano (*not* Cy'rano)
'Jodelet
Lig'nière
'Montfleury (*not* Mont'fleury)
'Ragueneau
Rox'ane

Further Reading

Edmond Rostand, *Cyrano de Bergerac*, edited by Jacques Truchet (Paris, Imprimerie Nationale, 1983). This is the standard edition, including much secondary material.

Edmond Rostand, *Cyrano de Bergerac*, edited by Patrick Besnier (Paris: Folio, 1983, 1999)

Cyrano de Bergerac: a heroic comedy in five acts by Edmond Rostand translated by Christopher Fry (London and New York: Oxford University Press, 1975. Reprinted with an introduction and notes by Nicholas Cronk, (Oxford: World's Classics, 1996)

Cyrano de Bergerac by Edmond Rostand translated and adapted for the stage by Anthony Burgess (London: Hutchinson, 1985)

Edmond Rostand's Cyrano de Bergerac: a new verse translation [into Scots] by Edwin Morgan (Manchester: Carcanet, 1992)

Cyrano de Bergerac, *Other Worlds: the comical history of the states and empires of the moon and the sun*, translated and introduced by Geoffrey Strachan (London and New York: Oxford University Press, 1965; reprinted London: New English Library, 1976)

Laurent Calvié, *Cyrano de Bergerac dans tous ses états* (Toulouse: Anacharsis, 2004). Includes various biographical accounts of Cyrano used by Rostand, and an introductory essay, 'Le mythe de Cyrano'

Alba della Fazia Amoia, *Edmond Rostand* (Boston: Twayne Publishers, 1978)

Peter France, *A New Oxford Companion to Literature in French* (Oxford: Clarendon Press, 1995). See entries for Alexandrine, Cyrano de Bergerac, Decadence, Libertins, Preciosity, Rostand, Symbolism, Unities.

Susan M. Lloyd, *The Man Who Was Cyrano: a life of Edmond Rostand, creator of Cyrano de Bergerac.* (Bloomington, Indiana: Unlimited Publishing, 2004)

John Lough, *An Introduction to Seventeenth-Century France* (London: Longmans, 1954)

—, *Paris Theatre Audiences in the Seventeenth and Eighteenth Centuries* (London: Oxford University Press, 1957)

Stephen Varick Dock, *Costume and Fashion in the Plays of Molière: a seventeenth-century perspective* (Geneva: Slatkine, 1992)

Cyrano de Bergerac

I wanted to dedicate this poem to the soul of
CYRANO. But as his soul has passed into you,
COQUELIN, the poem too is yours.

E. R.

DRAMATIS PERSONAE

CYRANO DE BERGERAC

CHRISTIAN DE NEUVILLETTE

COMTE DE GUICHE

RAGUENEAU

LE BRET

CAPTAIN CARBON DE CASTEL-JALOUX

CADETS

LIGNIÈRE

VALVERT

FIRST MARQUIS

SECOND MARQUIS

THIRD MARQUIS

MONTFLEURY

BELLEROSE

JODELET

CUIGY

BRISSAILLE

BUSYBODY

FIRST MUSKETEER

SECOND MUSKETEER

SPANISH OFFICER

LIGHT-HORSEMAN

THEATRE DOORMAN

BOURGEOIS

HIS SON

PICKPOCKET

SPECTATOR

GUARD

PIPER

MONK

TWO MUSICIANS

PAGES

POETS

BAKERS

ROXANE

SISTER MARTHA

LISE

ORANGE-GIRL

MOTHER MARGARET OF JESUS

DUENNA

SISTER CLAIRE

ACTRESS

SOUBRETTE

FLOWER-GIRL

Crowd: bourgeois, *marquises, musketeers, pickpockets, bakers, poets, Gascon cadets, actors, musicians, pages, children, soldiers, Spaniards, men and women of the audience,* précieuses, *actresses, middle-class wives, nuns, etc.*

ACT I

A PERFORMANCE AT THE HOTEL DE BOURGOGNE

Scene: the Hotel de Bourgogne,[1] in 1640. The theatre is a former indoor tennis court, converted and decorated for stage performances.

The auditorium is oblong in shape; it is seen from an angle, so that one of its long sides runs from downstage L to upstage R, where it joins the fictitious stage. This stage is encumbered on both sides with seating. Two tapestries, which can be pulled aside, form its curtain. Above the stage, the Royal Arms. There are broad steps down from the stage to the auditorium. On either side of these steps, seats for the band of violins. A row of candles for foot-lights.

On either side of the auditorium there are galleries on two levels: the higher one is divided into boxes. No seats in the pit, except at the back (downstage L) where there are some benches arranged in tiers, and under a staircase leading to the upper galleries, of which we can see only the lower steps, a kind of little counter decorated with candles, flowers in vases, crystal glasses, decanters, plates of cakes, etc.

In the middle of the wall facing us, under the galleries, is the entrance to the theatre: a large door which keeps opening and closing to admit the audience. On either side of this door, here and there elsewhere in the theatre and above the counter, are posters printed in red bearing the title La Clorise.[2]

As the curtain rises, the auditorium is still in half-

darkness and almost empty. The chandeliers are resting on the floor of the pit, waiting to be lighted.

Scene I

THE AUDIENCE, *arriving in dribs and drabs*, GENTLE-MEN, *BOURGEOIS*, FOOTMEN, PAGES, PICKPOCKETS, DOORMAN, *etc. Then* NOBLEMEN, CUIGY, BRISSAILLE, ORANGE-GIRL, VIOLINS, *etc.*

Voices off, a gentleman enters running, followed by DOORMAN

DOORMAN

Hey! That'll be fifteen sous!

GENTLEMAN

Not me!

DOORMAN

Oh? And why not?

GENTLEMAN

King's Household. We don't pay.

DOORMAN [*to another gentleman*]

Hey! You!

SECOND GENTLEMAN

Musketeer. We get in free.

FIRST GENTLEMAN

Oh, there you are.
The play doesn't start till two. The place is empty.
Let's practise a few moves.
[*They fence with foils they have brought with them.*]

FOOTMAN [*entering*]

Hey, Flanquin!

SECOND FOOTMAN [*already there*]

Yes?

FIRST FOOTMAN

Look, I've got cards. Let's play.

SECOND FOOTMAN
                                        All right.
    [*They sit down.*]
FIRST FOOTMAN
    I stole a bit of candle from my master.
    [*Lights candle and sticks it on the ground.*]
GUARD [*to a* FLOWER-GIRL]
    You came before the lights were lit: that's nice.
    [*Puts his arm round her waist.*]
ONE OF THE FENCERS
    Touché!
ONE OF THE GAMBLERS
            Clubs!
GUARD
                    Just one kiss! Please!   10
FLOWER-GIRL
    They'll see us!
GUARD [*pulling her into a dark corner*]
                    No they won't, not over here!
A MAN [*sitting on the floor, beginning to unpack food*]
    That's good, we're early, plenty of time for our
        picnic.
BOURGEOIS [*arriving with his son*]
    Sit here, my boy.
GAMBLER
                    Three aces.
ANOTHER MAN [*taking a bottle from under his cloak and
    also sitting down*]
                            I always say
    There's no place to drink burgundy like the Burgundy!
BOURGEOIS
    Dear, dear, what a disreputable place!
    Drinkers, fighters, gamblers . . .
GUARD
                            Just one kiss!
BOURGEOIS
    Good Lord! To think that this is where Rotrou

Staged his great tragedies!

SON

And Corneille too!

PAGES [*enter, dancing in a line*]
Tra la la la la la lero lay!

DOORMAN
Now boys, none of your tricks!

FIRST PAGE

20   What, us sir? No sir!

[*To his friend*]
Got any string?

SECOND PAGE
Yes, and a fish-hook!

FIRST PAGE
Great, we can go up there and fish for wigs.

PICKPOCKET [*with a group of disreputable-looking young men*]
Now lads, pay attention: this is your first time,
You've a lot to learn.

SECOND PAGE [*calling up to other boys in the upper galleries*]
Pea-shooters?

THIRD PAGE [*above*]

Yes, and peas!

[*He peppers those below.*]

SON
What's the play, father?

BOURGEOIS
Clorise.

SON

And the author?

BOURGEOIS
Balthasar Baro. That's what you call a play.

PICKPOCKET
See the lace on their boot-tops? You cut that.

MAN IN AUDIENCE [*showing his friend a seat in the gallery*]
Look, the first night of the Cid,[1] I was up there!

PICKPOCKET [*miming the gesture of stealing one*]
Watches . . .
BOURGEOIS
                    You'll see some splendid actors here tonight . . .
PICKPOCKET
Handkerchiefs . . .
BOURGEOIS
                         Montfleury . . .
VOICE [*from the gallery*]
                                        Lights! We need light!   30
BOURGEOIS
Bellerose, l'Espy, Jodelet, Mistress Beaupré!
A PAGE [*in the pit*]
Oh good, here's the orange-girl!
ORANGE-GIRL [*appearing behind her counter*]
                              Oranges, gentlemen,
Raspberry cordial, syllabub . . .
FALSETTO VOICE
                              Out of my way!
FOOTMAN [*surprised*]
Marquises?² In the pit?
ANOTHER FOOTMAN
                         They won't stay long.
    [*Enter a group of foppish young noblemen.*]
A MARQUIS [*seeing the auditorium half empty*]
What, are we here first? No one to notice us?
No one to clamber over? That won't do!
    [*Seeing some friends*]
Cuigy! Brissaille!
    [*They embrace and kiss.*]
CUIGY
              At last a human face!
My dear, we're here before the lights are lit!
MARQUIS
I know, it's frightful, shall we go away?
SECOND MARQUIS
No, my lord, look – here comes the taper-man.

AUDIENCE

40   Ah! . . .

*[They gather round the chandeliers as they are lit. There
are now some people in the galleries.* LIGNIÈRE *enters
the pit, arm in arm with* CHRISTIAN DE NEUVILLETTE.
LIGNIÈRE *is elegantly drunk, his clothes somewhat dis-
ordered.* CHRISTIAN, *dressed carefully but not in the latest
fashion, seems preoccupied and keeps looking up at the
boxes.]*

Scene II

As Scene I, plus CHRISTIAN, LIGNIÈRE, *then* RAGUENEAU
and LE BRET

CUIGY
   Lignière!
BRISSAILLE [*laughing*]
                  Not drunk yet?
LIGNIÈRE [*to* CHRISTIAN, *sotto voce*]
                        Shall I introduce you?
   [CHRISTIAN *nods.*] Gentlemen, the Baron de Neuvillette.
AUDIENCE [*as the first chandelier is raised*]
                                                          Ah!

LIGNIÈRE [*to* CHRISTIAN, *introducing them*]
   Baron, Messieurs de Cuigy, de Brissaille.
CHRISTIAN [*bowing*]
   Your servant, sirs.
FIRST MARQUIS [*to the second*]
                  Quite pretty, I suppose,
   But sadly out of fashion.
LIGNIÈRE [*to* CUIGY]
                        Our young friend
   Has just arrived in Paris.
CHRISTIAN
                        Yes, from Touraine,

I've come to join the Guards. I start tomorrow,
In the cadets.
FIRST MARQUIS [*studying the boxes*]
                    Look, there's my lady Aubrey.
ORANGE-GIRL
Oranges, syllabub . . .
CUIGY
                    Here they come!
CHRISTIAN
                                        Who?
FIRST MARQUIS
Why, everyone . . . well, everyone who matters.   50
[*Waving and smiling, they name each elaborately dressed
lady as she enters her box.*]
SECOND MARQUIS
Mesdames de Guémené . . .
CUIGY
                    De Bois-Dauphin . . .
BRISSAILLE
De Chavigny . . .
SECOND MARQUIS
                    The heart-breaker . . .
LIGNIÈRE
                                        I say,
There's Monsieur Corneille, all the way from Rouen.
BOY
Is that the Academy,[1] father?
BOURGEOIS
                    Quite a few of them;
There's Boudu, Boissat, Cureau de la Chambre,
Porchères, Colomby, Bourzeys, Boudon, Arbaud . . .
All of those names, sure of eternal fame . . .
FIRST MARQUIS
Look, here come all the literary ladies!
Barthénoïde, and there's Urimédonte,
Félixérie . . .
SECOND MARQUIS [*overcome*]
                    Such wonderful *noms de plume*![2]   60

Do you know them all, sir?

FIRST MARQUIS

                              Sir, I believe I do.

LIGNIÈRE [*taking* CHRISTIAN *aside*]

Dear boy, I came to help you with the lady,
But she's not here, and so I'll take my leave.

CHRISTIAN

No! Stay! You have to tell me who she is.
I love her so!

THE LEADER OF THE VIOLINS [*striking his desk with his
    bow*]

                    Attention, gentlemen!

ORANGE-GIRL

Macaroons! Lemonade!
    [*The violins begin to play.*]

CHRISTIAN

                          I'm frightened.
I'm sure she's clever, one of those *précieuses*[3]
Who talks the latest language – when I hear it
I just clam up. Fighting is more my line.
She always sits at the end there, on the right
Where the empty seats are.

LIGNIÈRE

                              I really must go.

CHRISTIAN

No, please stay!

LIGNIÈRE

                    I said I'd meet d'Assoucy[4]
For a drink. I'm dying of thirst here.

ORANGE-GIRL [*passing with a tray*]

                                    Orangeade?

LIGNIÈRE

Ugh!

ORANGE-GIRL

    Milk?

LIGNIÈRE

          Worse!

70

ORANGE-GIRL
                        White wine?
LIGNIÈRE
                                        Perhaps
I'll stay a little longer. Wine, you say . . . ?
[*He sits down near the buffet. The* ORANGE-GIRL *pours him some wine. Cries from the crowd as a little fat man appears.*]
CROWD
Here's Ragueneau!
LIGNIÈRE [*to* CHRISTIAN]
                        The famous Ragueneau.
RAGUENEAU [*a pastry-cook dressed in his best, rushing up to* LIGNIÈRE]
Oh sir, has Monsieur Cyrano been here?
LIGNIÈRE [*to* CHRISTIAN]
Pastry-cook to the stars!
RAGUENEAU
                                Sir, you're too kind.
LIGNIÈRE
Admit it, you're a patron of the arts.
RAGUENEAU
Some of the writing gentlemen do come . . .   80
LIGNIÈRE
And fill their bellies in your shop – on tick.⁵
You write yourself . . .
RAGUENEAU
                        Sometimes . . .
LIGNIÈRE
                                        Verse, I believe.
RAGUENEAU
Verse! I adore it, sir! Surely an ode . . .
LIGNIÈRE
Is worth an apple tart . . .
RAGUENEAU [*apologetically*]
                        Only a tartlet!
LIGNIÈRE
Don't be ashamed! I've heard that for a sonnet . . .

RAGUENEAU
  I sometimes give a bun . . .
LIGNIÈRE [*sternly*]
                                    With icing on it.
  And what about the theatre?
RAGUENEAU
                                    My passion!
LIGNIÈRE
  How do you buy your tickets then, with cakes?
  What did you pay today?
RAGUENEAU
                                    Fifteen cream puffs.
  [*Looking about him*]
90 But where is Cyrano? He should be here.
LIGNIÈRE
  Why?
RAGUENEAU
      Montfleury's on tonight.
LIGNIÈRE
                                    That's right.
  The mighty tub of lard is playing Phaedo.
  But what is that to Cyrano?
RAGUENEAU
                                    Don't you know?
  He's taken a spite to Montfleury, and told him
  He's not to show his face on stage all month.
LIGNIÈRE
  Ah!
RAGUENEAU
  And tonight, Montfleury plays the lead.
CUIGY [*who has joined them*]
  What can Cyrano do to stop him? Nothing.
RAGUENEAU
  Nothing? We'll see.
FIRST MARQUIS
                Who is this Cyrano?

CUIGY

A fair hand with a broadsword.

SECOND MARQUIS

Is he a gentleman?

CUIGY

Well, up to a point. A cadet[6] in the Guards. 100

[*Indicating a gentleman who seems to be looking for someone*]

But here's his friend Le Bret. I say, Le Bret!

Are you looking for Bergerac?

LE BRET

Yes, have you seen him?

CUIGY

Tell us, isn't he someone quite unusual?

LE BRET

Oh, he's the most remarkable man you'll ever . . .

RAGUENEAU

A poet!

CUIGY

Swordsman!

BRISSAILLE

Natural philosopher!

LE BRET

Musician!

LIGNIÈRE

And his looks – extraordinary!

RAGUENEAU

Philippe de Champaigne[7] will never paint him, that's true.

He's more like one of Callot's[8] extravagant captains.

With his three-plumed hat and six skirts to his doublet,

The set of his sword behind him lifting his cloak 110

Like a rooster's tail, his stiff-starched Spanish ruff –

He's the proudest Gascon[9] alive – and then his nose!

You wait to see him take it off, but no,

The thing is real and he's proud of it.

LE BRET

He'll fight with anyone who comments on it.

RAGUENEAU [*proudly*]
His blade snip-snaps, sharp as the shears of Fate.

FIRST MARQUIS
He won't come.

RAGUENEAU
                              He will, you know. I'll bet
One of my special chickens.

FIRST MARQUIS [*laughing*]
                                        Done!

CROWD
                                          Oh, look!
[*A murmur of admiration runs through the theatre.*
ROXANE *has just appeared in her box. She sits at the*
front, her duenna behind her. CHRISTIAN *is paying the*
ORANGE-GIRL *and has not noticed.*]

SECOND MARQUIS
Oh, isn't she beautiful! What a complexion!

FIRST MARQUIS
Peaches and cream, with a strawberry smile!

SECOND MARQUIS
120   And so cool
That near at hand, your heart might catch a chill.

CHRISTIAN [*raises his head, sees* ROXANE *and grabs*
      LIGNIÈRE's *arm*]
There she is!

LIGNIÈRE
                        Oh, is that her?

CHRISTIAN
                                  Yes, who is she?
Quickly, I'm trembling.

LIGNIÈRE
                              Madeleine Robin,
Known as Roxane. A *précieuse*.

CHRISTIAN
                                  No hope for me, then!

LIGNIÈRE
Spinster, an orphan, cousin to Cyrano –
The man we were speaking of . . .

[*A nobleman, very elegantly dressed, wearing the blue cordon of a knightly order, is now standing in the box talking to* ROXANE.]

CHRISTIAN

                                        There, is that him?

LIGNIÈRE

                                                        No!

That's the Comte de Guiche. He's mad for her,
But his wife's the Cardinal's niece. And so he'd like
To see her married off to one Valvert –
A viscount, but he'd still turn a blind eye.   130
She doesn't want the marriage, but De Guiche
Has power to persecute a mere *bourgeoise*.
I wrote a song about it – let me see –
Such a cruel ending . . .
      [*He rises unsteadily to his feet and raises his glass, ready to begin singing.*]

CHRISTIAN

                        No, not now. Goodnight.

LIGNIÈRE

Where are you going?

CHRISTIAN

                        To find Monsieur de Valvert.

LIGNIÈRE

And kill him. I see. What if he kills you?
Don't go, she's looking at you.

CHRISTIAN

                              So she is!
      [*He gazes at her, oblivious of everything else. Seeing their opportunity, the pickpockets move towards him.*]

LIGNIÈRE

I'll be off now, I'm thirsty and my friends
Are in the wine-shop.

LE BRET [*having inspected the whole auditorium, returns to*
      RAGUENEAU, *saying confidently*]
                        No sign of Cyrano.

RAGUENEAU [*not convinced*]
That's strange!

LE BRET

140   Please God he didn't see the playbill!

AUDIENCE [*starting to become restive*]
We want the play!

Scene III

SAME ACTORS, *minus* LIGNIÈRE, DE GUICHE, VALVERT
and presently MONTFLEURY

DE GUICHE *leaves* ROXANE's *box and crosses the pit,
followed by a gaggle of obsequious gentlemen, including*
VALVERT.

A MARQUIS
                    De Guiche isn't short of friends.

ANOTHER
Another Gascon!

THE FIRST ONE
                    Yes, the successful sort:
Clever and cold. We'd better pay our respects.
    [*They approach* DE GUICHE.]
What handsome ribbons! What's the colour, sir?[1]
Doe's-belly fawn, or is it Kiss-me-sweet?

DE GUICHE
It's Faint-heart Spaniard.

FIRST MARQUIS
                    How appropriate,
Since Spanish hearts must fail as you advance.
Flanders will soon be ours.

DE GUICHE [*moving towards the stage, followed by his
    gentlemen*]
                    Come, Valvert.

CHRISTIAN
                                        Valvert!
Time to throw down the gauntlet!

[*He reaches into his pocket and finds himself clutching the hand of a* PICKPOCKET.]
                                            Hey!
PICKPOCKET
                                            Ow!
CHRISTIAN
Where's my glove!
PICKPOCKET
                            That's not a glove, it's my hand.   150
Let me go, sir, please, and I'll tell you a secret.
CHRISTIAN [*keeping hold of him*]
What secret?
PICKPOCKET
                    Your friend Lignière is in trouble.
You know that song he wrote about someone important?
Well, his lordship wasn't too pleased, and to teach him a
    lesson
He's stationed a hundred men at the Porte de Nesle.[2]
I was supposed to be one of them.
CHRISTIAN
                                    Lignière in danger!
PICKPOCKET
You could say that.
CHRISTIAN [*finally letting go of him*]
                            But where can I find him?
PICKPOCKET
Try all the wine-shops: the Golden Press, the Funnels,
The Three Tuns, the Pine-Cone, the Two Torches,
Leave him a message . . .
CHRISTIAN
                        I'll do it. I'll go at once.   160
The villains! A hundred men against one!
    [*Looking fondly at* ROXANE]
But Roxane! How can I leave her?
    [*Glaring at* VALVERT]
                                    And him? But I must.
I have to rescue Lignière.
    [*Exit* CHRISTIAN, *running.* DE GUICHE, VALVERT, *the*

MARQUISES *and all the gentlemen have disappeared behind the curtain to take their seats on the stage. The pit is full and there are no more seats in the galleries or the boxes.*]

AUDIENCE

The play! The play!

[*The* PAGES *fishing from the gallery have managed to catch the wig of an elderly* BOURGEOIS.]

BOURGEOIS

My wig!

AUDIENCE

Look at that! Ha, ha! He's bald as a coot! Well done, boys!

BOURGEOIS [*shaking his fist*]

You little devils, wait till I catch you . . .

AUDIENCE [*loudly at first, then decrescendo to complete silence*]

Ha,

Ha, ha . . .

LE BRET

Why the silence?

[*A member of the audience whispers to him.*]

Oh, is he?

AUDIENCE MEMBER

Somebody told me.

AUDIENCE VOICES

Shh! . . . Is he here? . . . No . . . Yes . . . Where? In that box behind the grille . . . The Cardinal's here![3]

PAGE

Damn it! That's the end of our fun for today.

[*Three knocks on the stage. The audience falls silent, expectant.*]

VOICE OF A MARQUIS [*behind the curtain*]

Put out that candle!

ANOTHER MARQUIS [*sticking his head out between the curtains*]

Pass me a chair!

AUDIENCE MEMBER
Quiet!
[*Three knocks again. The curtain opens, revealing the noblemen slouching in chairs on either side of the stage. The backdrop is a pastoral scene; the stage is lit by four small chandeliers and the violins are playing quietly.*]

LE BRET [*sotto voce, to* RAGUENEAU]
Does Montfleury come on soon?

RAGUENEAU
Yes, he speaks first.

LE BRET
I don't see Cyrano.

RAGUENEAU
So I lose my bet.

LE BRET
Thank God for that.
[*Rustic music. Enter* MONTFLEURY *in the costume of a shepherd of pastoral. Immensely fat, he is wearing, at a rakish angle, a hat adorned with a garland of roses and carrying a beribboned set of bagpipes.*]

AUDIENCE [*clapping*]
Montfleury! Here he comes!

MONTFLEURY [*acknowledges their applause, then speaks*]
How happy he who far from cities' strife
In woodland shades lives out a peaceful life
And there, unmindful of the tempest's rage . . .

A VOICE FROM THE PIT
Fool, have I not forbidden you the stage?
[*The audience is astonished. Everyone looks around to see where the voice is coming from.*]

AUDIENCE VOICES
What's going on? Who's that?
[*People in the boxes are standing up to try to see.*]

CUIGY
It's him!

LE BRET [*horrified*]
Cyrano!
How can we stop him?

THE VOICE
                        Miserable clown,
    Out of my sight!
AUDIENCE
                    Shame!
MONTFLEURY
                          But . . .
THE VOICE
180   You won't step down?
VARIOUS VOICES [*from the boxes and the pit*]
    Quiet! . . . Sit down! . . . Speak up, Montfleury!
MONTFLEURY [*hesitantly*]
    How happy he, who far from cities' . . .
THE VOICE
                                Well,
    What are you waiting for, Prince Florizel?
    Must I come up and cudgel your fat frame?
    [*Above the heads in the pit, a hand can be seen brandishing
    a walking stick.*]
MONTFLEURY [*in an ever fainter voice*]
    How happy he . . .
THE VOICE
                    Begone!
MONTFLEURY [*choking*]
                              . . . who far from strife . . .
CYRANO [*rising from the midst of the audience, standing on a
    chair, his hat at a martial angle, his moustache bristling,
    his nose ferocious*]
    This is too much!
    [*Sensation.*]

Scene IV

SAME ACTORS, *presently joined by* BELLEROSE *and*
JODELET

MONTFLEURY
                    Gentlemen, you must help me!
A MARQUIS [*unworried*]
    Go on, go on!
CYRANO
                    Listen, you great buffoon,
    Your cheeks are just too tempting: one more word
    I'll see they get the spanking they deserve.
THE MARQUISES
    Really!
CYRANO
                    Gentlemen, silence on the stage   190
    Or I'll let loose my cane among your ribbons.
ALL THE MARQUISES [*rising to their feet*]
    How dare you! . . . Montfleury . . .
CYRANO
                                    Let him go home,
    Before I make a cut-work of his guts.
A VOICE
    But . . .
CYRANO
            Away with him!
ANOTHER VOICE
                            But surely . . .
CYRANO
                                            Still here?
    Then there's no help for it, my sword must out
    And puncture this inflated sack of gout.
MONTFLEURY [*pulling the rags of his dignity about him*]
    Sir, 'tis the Muse that you insult in me.
CYRANO [*with great politeness*]
    Sir, had the Tragic Muse e'er heard your name,

Hearing you speak she'd wonder at your fame.
200   And then, methinks, on seeing you so wide
She'd plant her buskin[1] in your fat backside.

AUDIENCE
Montfleury! Montfleury! We want the play!

CYRANO [*to them*]
Who else would like to see my blade at work?

AUDIENCE [*drawing back*]
No need for that . . .

CYRANO [*to* MONTFLEURY]
      Leave the stage!

AUDIENCE [*drawing nearer and muttering*]
         Oh!

CYRANO [*turning round suddenly*]
        Someone not happy?

[*They retreat again.*]

A VOICE [*from the back of the pit, singing, to the tune of
'Lillibulero'*]
Who is Cyrano to say
That we cannot see the play?
Stop the interruptions, please,
And let them show us *La Clorise*!

AUDIENCE
La Clorise! *La Clorise*!
210   Let them show us *La Clorise*!
La Clorise! *La Clorise*!
All we want is *La Clorise*!

CYRANO
You wretches, if I hear that song once more
I'll kill the lot of you.

A *BOURGEOIS*
      Do you think you're Samson?

CYRANO
Lend me your jawbone,[2] sir, and we shall see.

A LADY [*in the boxes*]
This is unheard of!

A GENTLEMAN
                          Shocking!
A *BOURGEOIS*
                                    Quite disgraceful!
A PAGE
  Isn't it fun!
THE PIT
                  Shh! . . . Montfleury! . . . Cyrano . . .
CYRANO
  Silence!
THE PIT [*going wild*]
                  Baa! Moo! Hee-haw! Bow-wow!
CYRANO
  I tell you . . .
A PAGE
                  Mee-ow!
CYRANO
                          I said, be silent.
I challenge every man here to a duel,   220
The whole pit. I'm making a list now.
Walk up, young heroes, there's a chance for everyone,
I'll take you each in turn, put up your hands
And take a number. Who'll be first? You, sir?
You? No? Well, this is disappointing.
No takers for death with honour. Why? I know,
You blush to look upon my naked blade.
Let's continue our talk.
    [*Turning back to the stage, where* MONTFLEURY *is still
    hovering*]
                          As I was saying,
I wish to see the stage freed of this rank imposthume,[3]
Or else . . .
    [*Hand on his sword-hilt*]
                  I'll lance it.
    [*Sits down on his chair, in the middle of the circle that has
    formed around him, then:*]
                          I'll clap three times, and then   230

Your great moon face will go into eclipse.

THE PIT [*amused*]

Ah!

CYRANO

One!

MONTFLEURY

I . . .

A VOICE [*from the boxes*]

Don't go! Stay!

THE PIT

Oh no, he won't! . . . Oh yes, he will!

MONTFLEURY

Gentlemen!

CYRANO

Two!

MONTFLEURY

I'm sure you'd all prefer . . .

CYRANO

Three!

[MONTFLEURY *instantly disappears, as if through a trap-door. A storm of laughter, whistles and boos.*]

AUDIENCE

Boo! Sss! He's frightened! Montfleury, come back!

CYRANO [*delighted, leaning back in his chair, legs crossed*]

I dare him to come back.

A *BOURGEOIS*

Speech! Where's the Prologue?[4]

[*Enter* BELLEROSE. *He comes forward and bows to the audience.*]

THE BOXES

Ah, here comes Bellerose.

BELLEROSE

Ladies and gentlemen . . .

THE PIT

No! We want Jodelet!

JODELET [*stand-up comedian's manner, nasal voice*]

Boys and girls . . .

THE PIT
                                        Hurrah
Jodelet's the man! Speak up, Jodelet!
JODELET
                                        Quiet!
That *mighty* actor Montfleury . . .
    [*Mimes a huge belly.*]
THE PIT
                                        He's scared!   240
JODELET
. . . has had to leave us . . .
THE PIT
                        Rubbish! Bring him back!
ONE PARTY
    No!
THE OTHER
        Yes!
A YOUNG MAN [*to* CYRANO]
                        But tell me, sir, why *do* you
Hate Montfleury so?
CYRANO [*still seated, politely*]
                        My dear young fellow,
I have two reasons, either of which alone
Would explain my aversion. First, he's a dreadful actor.
He shouts his words, and puffs and blows between them
As if each line were a porter's load to carry
And not an airy thing with wings of its own.
And then – but that's my private quarrel.
THE OLD BOURGEOIS [*from behind him*]
                                        But sir,
Baro's *Clorise*, why won't you let us hear it?   250
CYRANO [*turning his chair towards the old man, in a respect-
    ful tone*]
Good sir, believe me, Baro's play is worthless.
It's my duty to interrupt it.
THE PRÉCIEUSES [*in the boxes*]
                        Oh! Outrageous!
Did you hear what he said? Poor Baro!

CYRANO [*turning towards the boxes, with a flourish*]
                                                    Dearest ladies!
Your beauty dazzles us, you haunt our dreams,
Death has no terrors if you smile on us.
Inspire our verses, please . . . but do not judge them.

BELLEROSE
We'll have to give them all their money back!

CYRANO
At last a sensible remark! Bellerose,
It never was my plan to starve the Muse.
    [*He stands up and throws a bag of money on to the stage.*]
Here, take this purse and let the matter rest.

AUDIENCE [*in admiration*]
                                                    Ahh! . . .

260

JODELET [*picking up the purse and weighing it in his hand*]
On these terms, sir, I'd agree to anything.
Stop our performance any day you like.

AUDIENCE
                                                    Boo!

JODELET
Even if you and I are hissed together.

BELLEROSE
Now we must ask you all to leave.

JODELET
                                                    All out!
[*The audience heads for the door, while* CYRANO *looks on
in satisfaction. But as the next scene develops, the crowd
stops moving. The ladies in the boxes, who had stood up
and put on their cloaks to leave, stop to listen and presently
sit down again.*]

LE BRET [*to* CYRANO]
Cyrano, this is mad.

A BUSYBODY [*approaching* CYRANO]
                                Montfleury! Shocking!
The Duc de Candale's his patron . . . Who is yours?

CYRANO
No one.

BUSYBODY
        No patron?
CYRANO
                        None.
BUSYBODY
                        How can that be?
No powerful name to stand between you and danger?
CYRANO
    I've told you twice: no. Must I say it a third time?
    I have no protector, sir –
        [*Putting his hand to his sword-hilt*]
                        just a protectress.⁵   270
BUSYBODY
    But you'll have to leave town . . .
CYRANO
                        Perhaps.
BUSYBODY
                                But the Duc de
        Candale . . .
CYRANO
    May have a lengthy reach, but mine . . .
        [*Showing his sword*]
                                . . . is longer.
BUSYBODY
    You surely don't imagine he would fight you.
CYRANO
    We'll see. But now, please go.
BUSYBODY
                        But . . .
CYRANO
                                Go, sir, quickly,
    Or tell me why you're staring at my nose.
BUSYBODY [*horrified*]
    I . . .
CYRANO
        Do you see something odd about it? Tell me.
BUSYBODY [*backing away*]
    No, not at all!

CYRANO
                    Is it limp? Does it dangle
Like an elephant's trunk? Is it hooked like the beak of an owl?
BUSYBODY
     I . . .
CYRANO
          A wart on the tip, perhaps, or a fly walking down it.
What *is* it that drew your attention?
BUSYBODY
                                        Nothing, I swear!
CYRANO
     Is my nose so remarkable?
BUSYBODY
                              No! I was doing
My best *not* to look at it.
CYRANO
                              Oh? Why?
BUSYBODY
                                        I'd heard . . .
CYRANO
     You think it's disgusting.
BUSYBODY
                              Of course not!
CYRANO
                                        Unhealthy.
BUSYBODY
     I beg you . . .
CYRANO
                    Its shape is obscene.
BUSYBODY
                                        What can you mean?
CYRANO
     Why then, dear sir, your air of disapproval?
Perhaps you think it is a touch too big.
BUSYBODY
     Why no, it's tiny, minuscule, a speck.

CYRANO
   What did you say? How dare you use such language!
   My nose a speck, indeed!
BUSYBODY
                              Oh, God!
CYRANO
                                  It's *huge*!
   My nose is huge, you wretched noseless wonder!   290
   This great proboscis is my pride and joy,
   Since a fine nose is the unfailing mark
   Of a fine man, witty, good-natured, brave,
   Courteous and forgiving, as I am myself,
   And you, you snub-nosed slug, will never be,
   Since that round featureless vacuity
   That sits atop your neck, waiting for me
   To strike it . . .
      [*A resounding slap*]
                     . . . is as destitute of pride,
   Of poetry, of colour, spark or genius,
   Of sumptuousness, in a word of Nose,   300
   As its twin which swells at the base of your spine
   Where my boot will presently find it!
      [*Takes him by the shoulders, turns him round and kicks
      him.*]
BUSYBODY
                              Help! Guards!
CYRANO
   If anyone has any observations
   To make about the centre of my face
   Please note that if he's of sufficient breeding
   I make my mark with steel and not with leather,
   And further up the torso, and in front.
DE GUICHE [*who has come down from the stage with his
      entourage of marquis*]
   This has gone on too long.
VALVERT
                           Indeed. He's tiresome.

DE GUICHE
  Won't anybody rid us of him?
VALVERT
                                   No one?
310 Just watch, my lord, how I shall deal with him.
       [*He walks towards* CYRANO, *who watches him calmly, and*
       draws himself up before him in a self-important attitude.]
     Your nose, sir, is . . . er, well, it's . . . very big.
CYRANO
  Very.
VALVERT
         Ha, ha!
CYRANO
              Is that all?
VALVERT
                                   What?
CYRANO
                                   No.
  No, it's not all. You're lacking in invention,
  Young man. You could have said so many things.
  You could have been aggressive, for example:
  'Good heavens, man, if I'd a nose like that
  I'd have it amputated right away!'
  Solicitous: 'But sir, how do you drink?
  Doesn't it trail in your glass?' Or else descriptive:
320 'It's a rock, it's a peak, it's a cape . . . No, not a cape,
  It's a peninsula!' Inquisitive:
  'Do tell me, what is that long container?
  Do you keep pens in it, or scissors?' Twee:
  'How darling of you to have built a perch
  For little birds to rest their tiny claws.'
  Facetious: 'When you smoke, do they call "Fire"?
  Do people think some chimney is alight?'
  Worried: 'Now do be careful, when you walk,
  That you don't overbalance on your face.'
330 Motherly: 'We must make a little parasol
  To shade it from the sun.' Perhaps pedantic:

'Only the creature, sir, which Aristophanes
Calls *Hippocampelephantocamelos*
Could carry such a weight of flesh and bone
Below its forehead.' Friendly, masculine:
'I say, old chap, is that the latest fashion?
It certainly would do to hang your hat on!'
Grandiloquent: 'Oh dread protuberance,
Say what rash wind would dare to make you sneeze?'
Dramatic: 'Make the Red Sea one nosebleed.'   340
Fanciful: 'Is it a conch-shell? Are you a Triton?'
Naive: 'Is it a monument? When does it open?'
Or deferential: 'Please accept my compliments:
A nose like that's a claim on our respect.'
Rustic: 'Call that a nose, bor? Thass a marrer,
A winnin' one an' all.' Or military:
'Enemy closing, cannon aim and fire!'
Practical: 'You could put it up for sale,
And advertise it as a monster bargain.'
Tragical: 'Oh, that this too, too solid nose   350
Would melt, thaw and dissolve itself into a dewdrop!'
These are the things, sir, that you could have said
Had you a modicum of wit or letters,
But wit – good Lord – you don't know what it is,
And letters, well . . . just four can sum you up
F-O-O-L. But . . .
Even if you had had the inspiration
To entertain this noble audience
With such ingenious fancies, you would never
Have managed to articulate a quarter   360
Of half of the beginning of the first one,
For while I sometimes choose to mock myself,
I don't accept such pleasantries from others.
DE GUICHE [*trying to lead the dumbstruck* VALVERT *away*]
Come along, my lord let it be.
VALVERT [*choking with rage*]
The arrogance! A wretched country squire
Who looks as if he'd just come back from hunting!

No feathers, ribbons, lace: not even gloves!⁶

CYRANO

My notion of distinction's rather different.
If I don't trick myself out like a Paris fop,
370   Don't think that I don't care how people see me.
I'd never go outdoors unwashed, with an insult
Hanging about me, or a speck of yellow
Stuck in the eye of my conscience, my honour crumpled
Or my principles drooping. No, when I walk abroad,
I bear a haughty plume of independence.
Everything shines about me: if I stand tall
It's not to flaunt my figure, but my soul.
My only ornament's my reputation;
My wit's as springy as my coiled moustache,
380   And when I walk, that ringing sound you hear
Is not my spurs, it's truth.

VALVERT

                                    But sir . . .

CYRANO

                                                    No gloves?
Imagine that! I did have one, an odd one,
Left over from a very ancient pair.
Where can it be? I know, I must have left it
In somebody's face.

VALVERT

                        Oaf! Clown! Provincial half-wit!

CYRANO [doffing his hat and bowing, as if VALVERT had just
    introduced himself]
How do you do? Hercule-Savinien
De Cyrano de Bergerac.
    [laughter.]

VALVERT [furious]

                        Buffoon!

CYRANO [as if feeling a sudden pain]
Ouch!

VALVERT [who had begun to leave, now turning back
    towards CYRANO]
        What's that he says?

CYRANO [*pulling a face*]
                              It's gone to sleep.
  I've got to get it moving.
VALVERT
                              What's the matter?
CYRANO
  My sword's got pins and needles.
VALVERT [*drawing his sword*]
                              Very well.   390
CYRANO
  Let's make the thing more interesting, shall we?
VALVERT [*contemptuously*]
  You talk like a poet.
CYRANO
                    Indeed, and I shall prove it.
  As we fight, I'll improvise a ballade – you know
  What a ballade is, I presume.
VALVERT
                              Of course.
CYRANO [*ignoring him*]
  A ballade has three stanzas, each of eight lines,
  And an envoi of four. I'll fence and compose at once,
  And on the last line, thrust home.
VALVERT
                              Nonsense.
CYRANO
                                        We'll see.
  [*declaiming*]
  'Ballade of Monsieur Cyrano's Encounter
  With a Paris Coxcomb.'
VALVERT
                              What is that, pray?
CYRANO
                                        The title.
AUDIENCE [*intensely excited*]
  Let's see! Move over! What are they doing now?   400
  [*There is now a circle of curious spectators in the pit,
  marquises and officers mingling with bourgeois and*

*working people. The pages have climbed on people's shoul-
ders to see the fun. In the boxes, all the ladies are standing
up.* DE GUICHE *and his gentlemen stage L,* LE BRET,
RAGUENEAU, CUIGY, *etc., stage R.*]

CYRANO [*closing his eyes for a moment*]
Wait! Let me choose my rhymes . . . That's it, I'm ready.
[*Suiting the action to the word*]
Nonchalantly I cast aside my hat,
Slowly unwind the cloak that wraps my frame.
Now draw my sword and, wary as a cat,
Circle the space that must enclose our game.
As challenger, my lord, you're much to blame:
Use in defence whatever moves you like,
I tell you now, the end will be the same,
And when my poem is complete, I'll strike.
[*They begin to fence.*]
410   Where shall I mark you first? Admitting that
My sword must pierce your skin, which spot to claim?
Beneath that nice protective layer of fat
Your heart, perhaps? The obvious point to aim . . .
But striking now would leave my stanza lame,
And I aspire to enjoy the two alike –
The deadly swordsman's and the poet's fame –
So when my poem is complete, I'll strike.

You're turning pale! The fathers that begat
You now must blush for you: the stately dame
420   Who was your mother – now, what rhymes with -at? –
Must turn away and hide her face for shame.
You never saw that movement as it came!
You're handling that fine rapier like a pike!
And giving me the leisure to proclaim
That when my poem is complete, I'll strike.

Prince, did they never tell you what became
Of self-admiring nobles who decry
Common adventurers? Now you know my name,
And now my poem is complete, *(thrusting)* I strike!

[VALVERT *staggers and falls. Cries of admiration. Applause from the boxes. Flowers and lace handkerchiefs rain down. The officers crowd around* CYRANO *to congratulate him.* RAGUENEAU *is dancing a jig with excitement.* LE BRET *does not know whether to laugh or cry.* VALVERT'S *friends carry him away.*]

A LIGHT CAVALRYMAN
  Superb!

A WOMAN
        Enchanting!

MARQUIS
                Most unusual!   430

LE BRET
  Insane!
    [*Everyone is gathering around* CYRANO.]

THE CROWD
        Congratulations! Wonderful!

A WOMAN
  A genuine hero!

A MUSKETEER
          Sir, may I shake your hand?
  I've some experience of these things, and that
  Was remarkable. Your servant. [*Bows and leaves.*]

CYRANO [*to* CUIGY]
                Who was that?

CUIGY
  His name is D'Artagnan.[7]

LE BRET [*taking* CYRANO *by the arm*]
                We have to talk.

CYRANO
  Let's wait here till the crowd has gone.
    [*To* BELLEROSE]
                May we?

BELLEROSE [*respectfully*]
  Of course, sir.
    [*A sound of booing outside.*]

JODELET [*having looked out*]
          Well! They're booing Montfleury.

BELLEROSE [*solemnly*]
  Sic transit gloria.[8]
    [*To* DOORMAN *and lamp-man, in an everyday voice*]
                              You can sweep up now,
  And close the doors. But leave some candles lit.
  We'll be rehearsing later, after dinner:
  The farce for tomorrow.
    [*Exeunt* BELLEROSE *and* JODELET, *bowing deeply to*
    CYRANO.]
DOORMAN [*to* CYRANO]
                                    Not dining, sir?
CYRANO
                                                      No.
                                          [*Exit* DOORMAN.]
LE BRET
  No dinner?
CYRANO [*proudly*]
      No.
    [*When he sees* DOORMAN *has gone*]
                  No money.
LE BRET [*miming throwing the purse*]
                              But the bag of gold?
CYRANO
  A month's allowance – gone!
LE BRET
                              So now you're starving.
  What a mad thing to do!
CYRANO
                              But what a gesture!
ORANGE-GIRL [*coughs discreetly.* CYRANO *and* LE BRET *turn
  to her. Then*]
  Sir, I can't bear to see you going hungry.
  I've some food here . . . Won't you . . .
CYRANO
                                          Dear child,
  My Gascon pride forbids me to accept
  The least thing from your dainty fingers – still,
  Rather than hurt your feelings by refusing,

440

I will take something – let me see – a grape.   450
ORANGE-GIRL
Oh, sir! Take the bunch!
CYRANO
               Thank you, no.
And a glass of your clear water –
   [*She tries to pour him wine.*]
                      no, water –
And half a macaroon.
LE BRET
              You're being silly.
ORANGE-GIRL
Take something more.
CYRANO
            I will – your hand to kiss.
[*Kisses it as ceremoniously as if she were a princess.*]
ORANGE-GIRL
Thank you, sir. Good night. [*Curtsies and leaves.*]

Scene V

CYRANO, LE BRET, *presently* DOORMAN

CYRANO
              Now, Le Bret, your advice.
[*Carefully placing in front of himself the macaroon*]
Here we have dinner . . .
   [*The glass of water*] wine . . .
           [*The grape*] dessert. Let's begin.
I must admit I was extremely hungry.
You were saying?
LE BRET
           Those duel-mad idiots!
Spend time with them and you'll become just like them.
Ask someone level-headed what impression   460
You made today.

CYRANO [*finishing his macaroon*]
                         I know: I was astounding.
LE BRET
    You think so, but the Cardinal . . .
CYRANO [*delighted*]
                                   Was *he* here?
LE BRET
    He must have been outraged . . .
CYRANO
                              Nonsense, he'll have loved it.
    He writes himself, you know: he'll hardly mind
    If someone else's play's booed off the stage.
LE BRET
    You're making still more enemies each day.
CYRANO [*nibbling his grape*]
    Really! How many this time, would you say?
LE BRET
    Forty-eight at least, not counting the women.
CYRANO
    Oh, but we must count *them*. Give me the list.
LE BRET
470   De Guiche, Valvert, Baro and Montfleury,
    That old *bourgeois*, the whole Academy . . .
CYRANO
    Wonderful!
LE BRET
                    Yes, but where will all this end?
    What are you aiming at?
CYRANO
                                I wasn't sure –
    I trifled with so many things – but now
    I know what I want.
LE BRET
                        And may one know the answer?
CYRANO
    Just to be admirable, nothing more.
LE BRET
    I see – but now we're alone, won't you tell me

What's the real reason you hate Montfleury so?
CYRANO
That fat Silenus,[1] with his bulging belly –
His arms aren't long enough to reach his navel –   480
Thinks he's God's gift to women: every time
He stands on stage there, posturing and wheezing,
He makes sheep's eyes at them out of his toad's face.
One night – and ever since I've hated him –
He let his eyes rest on the woman . . . Ugh!
It made me think of a great slimy slug
Crawling along a petal.
LE BRET
                    What! You?
No! Cyrano in love!
CYRANO [sadly]
                    I'm afraid so, yes.
LE BRET
You never told me! Why not?
CYRANO
                    Look at me.
Who in the world could love a face like this?   490
My nose goes everywhere ahead of me!
And yet I love – inevitably – who?
The most beautiful woman in Paris.
LE BRET
                    In Paris?
CYRANO
                    The world!
The loveliest, cleverest, daintiest – blondest – of all.
LE BRET
Just tell me, who is she?
CYRANO
                  A dangerous innocent,
A budding rose between whose folded petals
Love lies in wait to trap us. Oh, her smile!
To look upon it is to know perfection.
Her slightest gesture has a god-like grace:
Carried through Paris in her chair, or walking,   500

She'd make a man forget the sea-borne Venus
Or brave Diana[2] striding through the woods.

LE BRET

I know! There's only one girl . . .

CYRANO

                                        Only one.

LE BRET

Your cousin, Madeleine Robin.

CYRANO

                                        Roxane.

LE BRET

But this is perfect! If you love her, tell her.
She must have been impressed with you this evening.

CYRANO

Open your eyes, Le Bret. What admiration
Could possibly survive the sight of my profile?
I know what I look like. Oh, I admit that sometimes
510   In springtime, in the perfume of a garden,
By moonlight, I may envy passing lovers
And dream of being like them. My heart melts –
And then I see my shadow on the wall.

LE BRET [*moved*]

Dear friend!

CYRANO

                Dear friend, indeed, it's sometimes painful
To feel myself so ugly, so alone . . .

LE BRET [*urgently, taking his hand*]

You're not crying?

CYRANO

                        No! What? Imagine
The sight of tears running down this great – *thing*!
I have respect for tears, they can be beautiful.
How can I mix them up with such absurdity?
520   Make people laugh at tears? I'd rather die.

LE BRET

Don't be so sad; perhaps you'll be lucky in love.

CYRANO

No. I love Cleopatra – am I Caesar?

Berenice is my passion – am I Titus?[3]

LE BRET

But your courage! Your wit! Even the orange-girl
Who was here just now – she couldn't take her eyes off
    you.

CYRANO [*struck by the idea*]

That's true.

LE BRET

            Well, then. Even Roxane turned pale
When she saw you in danger today.

CYRANO

                        Pale! Are you sure?

LE BRET

Yes, it's plain that she cares about you. Be brave
And speak to her.

CYRANO

             Yes, and make her laugh at me! That's
The only thing I'm afraid of.

DOORMAN [*leading a woman towards* CYRANO]

                Excuse me, sir,   530

A lady to see you.

CYRANO

            Oh heavens, it's her duenna!

Scene VI

CYRANO, LE BRET, DUENNA

DUENNA [*bowing*]

My lady's greeting to her gallant cousin.
She begs the favour of a private meeting.

CYRANO

With me?

DUENNA [*curtsying*]

          With you, sir. She has things to tell you.

CYRANO
    Things?
DUENNA [*curtsying again*]
            Things.
CYRANO [*almost fainting*]
                    Can it be?
DUENNA
                            At dawn tomorrow
    My lady will be at St Roch's – first mass.
CYRANO [*leaning on* LE BRET]
    God help me!
DUENNA
                Then, do you know a place to go
    To have a private talk, just for a moment?
CYRANO
    To talk . . . why yes . . . oh, heavens! . . . let me think . . .
DUENNA
    Quickly!
CYRANO
            I know . . .
DUENNA
                        Where?
CYRANO
540   At Ragueneau's.
DUENNA
    And who is Ragueneau?
CYRANO
                        The pastry-cook.
    There, in the rue – the rue Saint-Honoré.
DUENNA
    We'll meet you there at seven. Don't forget.
CYRANO [*aside*]
                            Forget!

Scene VII

CYRANO, LE BRET, *followed by* ACTORS, ACTRESSES,
CUIGY, BRISSAILLE, LIGNIÈRE, DOORMAN, MUSICIANS

CYRANO [*falling into* LE BRET'S *arms*]
She wants to see me.
LE BRET
                                   Not so sad now, eh?
CYRANO
What can she want? Who cares? She knows I exist.
LE BRET
So now, will you be sensible?
CYRANO
                                   Sensible!
I'll be totally wild! I could fight a whole army!
[*At the top of his voice*]
My heart is ready to burst! My arm's a giant's!
[*On the unlit stage actors and actresses are beginning to
move about and whisper: the rehearsal is about to begin.
The musicians have taken up their positions again.*]
A VOICE [*from the stage*]
Hey! Quiet, everybody! We're rehearsing!
CYRANO [*laughing*]
We're going.
[*As he begins to leave, the main door opens. Enter* CUIGY,
BRISSAILLE *and several officers, holding up* LIGNIÈRE,
who is totally drunk.]
CUIGY
                    Cyrano!
CYRANO
                                   What?
CUIGY
                                   Someone to see you.   550
He's had a few drinks.
CYRANO
                              Lignière! What's the matter?

BRISSAILLE
  He can't go home.
CYRANO
                        Why not?
LIGNIÈRE [*slurring his words, showing him a tattered note*]
                        Got this note . . .
  Danger . . . a hundred men . . . Song I wrote . . .
  All at the Porte de Nesle, can't go home that way . . .
  Bit of a problem . . . Can I stay with you?
CYRANO
  A hundred men, you say? We'll see you home.
LIGNIÈRE [*alarmed*]
  But . . .
CYRANO [*in a fearsome voice, pointing to the lantern which*
  DOORMAN *is holding as he looks on curiously*]
                Take the lantern. Walk. I'll be behind you.
  [*To the officers*]
  You, you can watch, but mind you keep your distance.
  A hundred men, that's what I need tonight!
    [*The actors and actresses, in costume, have come down
    from the stage and now draw nearer.*]
LE BRET
  But why . . .
CYRANO
560   Good old Le Bret, always complaining!
LE BRET
  Why risk your life for a drunk you hardly know?
CYRANO
  I saw him once do something really striking.
  One day at mass he saw the girl he loved
  Take holy water – water's a thing he hates,
  And yet he ran to the font and drank it dry!
ACTRESS [*in soubrette costume*]
  Yes, that was something!
CYRANO
                        Wasn't it, my dear?
ACTRESS
  But why a hundred men against one poet?

CYRANO
  Let's go.
  [*To the officers*] Whatever you may see me do
  I solemnly forbid you to assist me.
ANOTHER ACTRESS [*jumping down from the stage*]
  I must see this.
CYRANO
                    Come along, then.
ANOTHER [*also jumping down and speaking to an old actor*]
                                        Coming, dear?   570
CYRANO
  Come, all of you, the Doctor, Isabelle,
  Léandre, everyone: your charming capers
  Will add Italian farce to a Spanish drama,
  A tinkling of silver bells to a dismal drum-beat
  Till we think we're dancing along to a tambourine.
ALL THE WOMEN [*dancing with delight*]
  Hurrah! Quickly! My cloak! My hood!
JODELET
                                        Let's go!
CYRANO [*to the musicians*]
  And you, gentlemen of the band, can play us out.
  [*The musicians join the column which is forming. Every-
  one takes candles from the footlights and passes them
  around, so that the cortège becomes a torchlight pro-
  cession.*]
CYRANO
  Excellent! Officers, women in costume, and –
  Twenty paces ahead – myself, alone,
  Under my glorious plume, thrice Nasica –[1]   580
  Alone, you understand, no one must help me –
  I lead the advance. All ready? Porter, the door!
  [DOORMAN *opens it wide, revealing a slice of Paris by
  moonlight.*]
  Paris is fading into night-time mists,
  Moonlight is flowing down the city rooftops,
  Under the coils of vapour shines the Seine,

Mysterious, trembling – let's give her something to tremble
    at!
To the Porte de Nesle!

ALL

                        To the Porte de Nesle!

CYRANO [*to the soubrette*]
    You asked what need to send a hundred men
    To punish one poor poet? I reply,
590   They knew that poet was a friend of mine.

ACT II

THE POETS' COOK-SHOP

RAGUENEAU's *cooked-meat and cake shop, at the corner of the rue St-Honoré and the rue de l'Arbre-Sec. The street, grey in the light of dawn, can be seen through a glass door downstage L.*

Downstage R, a counter with above it a metal frame supporting geese, ducks and white peacocks, all still in the feather. On the counter, tall vases of brightly coloured flowers, chiefly sunflowers. Behind the counter, a huge fireplace. Soup pots standing on the fire-dogs and a row of roasts already weeping into the dripping pans.

Downstage L, above the door, a flight of stairs leading to a little upper room, the inside of which can be seen through open shutters. A table has been laid: above it hangs a small Flemish candelabra. Favoured customers can eat and drink there. A wooden gallery, connecting with the stair, seems to lead to other similar rooms.

In the middle of the shop, carcasses of game are hanging from a large round metal rack, which can be raised and lowered by a pulley – a kind of game chandelier.

Upstage the ovens are already red; copper pots are gleaming, spits turning, hams hanging from the rafters. Elaborate desserts tower on dishes. It is the morning rush. Anxious underlings are running about, among enormous cooks and tiny scullions. Many have a pheasant's feather or a chicken's wing in their caps. On sheet-metal trays or long wicker baskets, boys are carrying symmetrical mounds of buns, whole villages of little cakes.

Some of the tables are covered in cakes and plates; others

*are already laid for the morning's customers. One little
table, in a corner, is piled high with papers.* RAGUENEAU
*is sitting at it, writing. His manner is that of an inspired
poet, and he is counting syllables on his fingers.*

Scene I

RAGUENEAU, COOKS, *then* LISE

FIRST COOK
   Marzipan fruits!
SECOND COOK
                   Flan!
THIRD COOK
                        Peacock!
FOURTH COOK
                              Mince pies!
RAGUENEAU [*lifting his pen*]
   Lo, how Dawn's rosy fingers gild the saucepans!
   Silence the god that speaks within thee, Ragueneau!
   The lyre will sing again, now to the stove!
      [*To one of the cooks*]
   This sauce is too reduced: lengthen it, please.
COOK
   By how much, sir?
RAGUENEAU
                   An iamb.
COOK
                         What?
FIRST BAKER
                              Tart, sir!
SECOND BAKER
                                   Cake, sir!
RAGUENEAU
   Hence, O my Muse, lest in your heavenly eyes
   The smoke of mortal cooking raise a tear!

[*To a baker, passing with loaves*]
Those loaves are ill-proportioned – the cesura[1]
Must cut them just in half – two hemistiches!   10
  [*To another, showing him a pie*]
This palace needs a roof –
  [*To a boy, loading chickens on a spit*]
                                        and on your spit,
The humble chicken and the stately turkey
Must take alternate places, as Malherbe[2]
Would alternate his rolling, mighty lines
With lighter ones: stanzas of poultry, that's it.

ANOTHER APPRENTICE
Sir, I made this for you, I hope you like it.

RAGUENEAU [*delighted*]
A lyre! In pastry! Stuck with candied fruits!

APPRENTICE
The strings are all spun sugar.

RAGUENEAU
                                        Excellent!
Here's a tip for you . . . Sh! Here comes your mistress!
Go, quickly, don't let her see it.
  [*To* LISE]
                                        Look, dear!   20
Isn't that beautiful?

LISE
                          It's absurd. Here,
I brought you your wrapping paper.

RAGUENEAU
                                        Thanks. Great heavens!
My precious books, dismembered, torn in pieces!
All my friends' verses, turned to bags for buns!
Murderess! Orpheus[3] was treated so!

LISE [*drily*]
Oh! So I'm not to use the only thing
Your rhyming friends have ever left behind them!

RAGUENEAU
Miserable ant! Those crickets sing divinely![4]

LISE
   Well, all I know is this: before they came
30   You never called me murderess – nor ant!
RAGUENEAU
   Turn poetry to paper bags!
LISE
                          That's right.
RAGUENEAU
   What do you do with prose, then?

Scene II

SAME ACTORS, *plus* TWO CHILDREN, *who have just come
into the shop.*

RAGUENEAU
                        Morning, children!
   What would you like today?
FIRST CHILD
                  Three pies, please.
RAGUENEAU
                             There!
   Nice and hot.
FIRST CHILD
            Will you wrap them for us?
RAGUENEAU
                        Wrap them?
   My precious verses! Wrap them, did you say?
   [*He takes a bag and, on the point of putting the pies in it,
   begins to read:*]
   Ulysses, as he left the Argive strand . . .
   Not that . . .
      [*Repeating the action with another bag*]
           As shining Phoebus . . . No, not that one . . .
LISE
   Ragueneau!

RAGUENEAU
            Just a minute! Just a minute!
    [*He takes a third bag, and this time fills it.*]
    The sonnet to Lucinda – but it's hard!
LISE
    At last!
    [*She turns her back and stands on a stool to put away
    some plates on a dresser.*]
RAGUENEAU [*to the children*]
            Psst! Bring me back the sonnet!   40
    I'll give you six pies – there! – instead of three!
    [*The children bring back the paper and run off with the
    pies.* RAGUENEAU *smooths it out and begins to read.*]
    Alas, Lucinda! – Grease on that sweet name!
    Alas, Lucinda! . . .

Scene III

RAGUENEAU, LISE, CYRANO, *then* MUSKETEER

CYRANO
                    What's the time?
RAGUENEAU
                                    Six o'clock.
CYRANO
    One hour from now!
RAGUENEAU
                    Congratulations!
CYRANO
                                            Why?
RAGUENEAU
    I saw you fight.
CYRANO
                    Fight? Where?
RAGUENEAU
                                    At the theatre.

CYRANO
Oh, that.
RAGUENEAU
Yes, the duel in verse.
LISE
He can't stop talking about it.
CYRANO
All the better.
RAGUENEAU
And when my poem is complete, I'll strike!
And when my poem is complete . . . Wonderful!
CYRANO
What time is it, Ragueneau?
RAGUENEAU

50
Five past six. – *I'll strike!*
LISE
What's wrong with your hand?
CYRANO
Nothing, just a scratch.
LISE
Was it really dangerous?
CYRANO
No . . .
LISE
Fibber!
CYRANO
What,
Is my nose growing? I don't see how it could.
Look, I'm expecting someone to meet me here –
When she comes, would you leave us alone?
RAGUENEAU
Sorry, I can't.
My friends will be here any moment – the poets, you know.
LISE
Come for their breakfast.
CYRANO
You can get rid of them, surely.

The time?
RAGUENEAU
       Ten past six.
CYRANO
              Lend me a pen?
RAGUENEAU
The quill of a swan, *cher maître.*
MUSKETEER [*enters swaggeringly*]
                   Morning all!
   [LISE *immediately moves towards him.*]
CYRANO
What's that?
RAGUENEAU
       Friend of the wife's . . . A warrior, *he* says.   60
CYRANO [*to* RAGUENEAU]
Shh!
[*To himself*]
   Write it . . . Fold it . . . Hand it to her . . . Run.
Coward! But still, I know I'd rather die
Than say a word . . . The time?
RAGUENEAU
                A quarter past . . .
CYRANO
A word of all the words I've got in there . . .
But if I wrote . . . Let's get it written, then,
This letter I've composed a hundred times,
Written and rewritten in my mind: it's ready
And all I have to do is lay my soul
Open beside the paper and copy it out.

Scene IV

RAGUENEAU, LISE, MUSKETEER, CYRANO *at the little
table, writing,* POETS, *dressed in black, slipshod and
muddy*

LISE
  Here's the hungry brigade!
FIRST POET
                                Brother!
SECOND POET
                                        Dear brother!
70
THIRD POET
  Swan of the cook-shop! Mm! Delicious smells!
FOURTH POET
  Phoebus of pastry!
FIFTH POET
                                Ovid of the ovens!
RAGUENEAU
  They treat me just like one of themselves!
FIRST POET
                                          We're late,
  There was such a crowd at the Porte de Nesle, all gaping
  At eight men, opened right up, blood everywhere.
CYRANO [*briefly interested*]
  Eight? I thought only seven.
RAGUENEAU
                                And who had killed them?
  Do you know, Cyrano?
CYRANO
                        No.
LISE [*to* MUSKETEER]
                        Do you?
MUSKETEER [*twirling his moustache*]
                                I might.
CYRANO [*writing*]
  I love you . . .

FIRST POET
                Well, they say a single swordsman
    Put the whole gang to flight.
SECOND POET
                                    You should have seen it –
    Pikes, staves all over the ground . . .
CYRANO
                                        Your eyes . . .   80
THIRD POET
    Hats strewn as far as the Quai des Orfèvres . . .
CYRANO
    And my heart fails me when I see your face . . .
SECOND POET
    Written anything lately, Ragueneau?
CYRANO
    Yours to command till death – no need to sign it,
    I'll give it to her myself.
RAGUENEAU
                        Nothing much –
    A recipe in verse.
THIRD POET [*eyeing a plate of cream buns*]
                        Oh, we must hear it!
FOURTH POET
    This bun has got its cap on at an angle. [*Bites it off.*]
FIRST POET
    This ginger man is ogling me, I'm sure.
        [*Plucks it from the plate.*]
SECOND POET
    The recipe.
THIRD POET [*gently squeezing a cream bun*]
                This cream's escaping – there!
SECOND POET [*biting into the pastry lyre*]
    Who said the Lyre would never feed us, eh?   90
RAGUENEAU [*drawing himself up and clearing his throat*]
    'A Rhyming Recipe . . .
SECOND POET [*nudging his neighbour*]
                        Breakfasting, what?

FIRST POET
    Dining, you mean, old chap!
RAGUENEAU
                                        . . . *for Almond Tartlets.*'
        First for the filling: almonds soaked in milk,
                                As soft as silk.
        Add them to eggs beaten as light as air
                                And waiting there.
        Cut up your short-crust paste and put it in
                                A tartlet tin.
        Press down each dainty round and neatly pour
100   A spoon or more
        Of almond mixture in each waiting nest.
                                Don't let them rest,
        But quickly to the oven bear the tray.
                                There it must stay
        For fifteen minutes. Then, like burnished gold,
                                Lo and behold,
        Your ALMOND TARTLETS!
THE POETS [*their mouths full*]
    Mm-mm! Delicious! Exquisite! Divine!
    [*They move upstage.*]
CYRANO [*to* RAGUENEAU]
    Can't you see how they're stuffing themselves?
RAGUENEAU
                                                    I know,
110   But they mustn't think I'm watching. I like to feed them,
    And it does give me a chance to read my verses.
CYRANO
    Well done!
        [RAGUENEAU *joins the poets upstage.* CYRANO *turns to*
        LISE *who is deep in conversation with* MUSKETEER.]
                            Lise, my dear, is that man annoying you?
LISE [*sulkily*]
    I can look after myself.
CYRANO
                            Make sure you do.
    I like your husband, and I don't intend

To see him made a fool of.
[*Loud enough for* MUSKETEER *to hear*]
                              Is that clear?
[MUSKETEER *salutes.* CYRANO *looks at the clock again,
then begins watching the door.*]
LISE [*to* MUSKETEER]
Are you going to let it go at that?
Say something to him – something about his nose.
MUSKETEER
His nose! You must be joking!
[*He beats a hasty retreat, followed by* LISE.]
CYRANO [*signalling to* RAGUENEAU *that it's time to get rid of
the poets*]
                                        Psst!
RAGUENEAU
                                        Gentlemen,
Shall we go inside? We can read our verses there.
FIRST POET [*anguished*]
But the cakes!
SECOND POET
                    The cakes!
THIRD POET
                    Let's take them with us.
RAGUENEAU
                                        Come!   120
[*They swoop on the remaining cakes, then, in procession,
follow* RAGUENEAU *out.*]

Scene V

CYRANO, ROXANE, DUENNA

CYRANO
I'll risk my letter if I think I have
The slightest hope.
  [DUENNA *and* ROXANE, *masked, appear at the window.*
  CYRANO *rushes to open the door.*]
      Ladies!
  [*Heading off* DUENNA]
         Madam, a word!
DUENNA [*flirtatiously*]
 Two.
CYRANO
    Are you fond of sweet things?
DUENNA
           I'm afraid so.
CYRANO [*picking up some papers*]
 Good. Here are two sonnets by Monsieur Benserade ...
DUENNA
 Oh dear!
CYRANO
    I'll fill them with tarts.
DUENNA
         That's better.
CYRANO
 What do you say to buns?
DUENNA
       Cream ones?
CYRANO
         Done!
Here we are, six of them, wrapped up neatly
In Saint-Amant's sonnets. Chapelain's[1] verse is heavy
But Ragueneau's pastry's light – try it, you'll see.
Fresh biscuits?

DUENNA
                    I adore them
CYRANO
                                    You can eat them   130
    Out in the street.
DUENNA
                    But sir, a lady . . .
CYRANO [*pushing her out of the door*]
                                    Thank you!
    And don't come back until you've scoffed the lot!
    [*He shuts the door, takes off his hat and stands at a respect-
    ful distance from* ROXANE.]

Scene VI

    CYRANO, ROXANE

CYRANO
    Blessed above all moments be the moment
    When, setting your forgetfulness aside,
    You finally admit that I exist,
    And come yourself to find me and to tell me,
    To tell me . . .
ROXANE
                    To thank you first of all. You know
    That man you fought with yesterday, that idiot
    You made a perfect fool of, he's the one
    A certain person who has noticed me . . .   140
CYRANO
    De Guiche?
ROXANE
                    Would like to see me marry.
CYRANO
    A marriage of convenience – *his* convenience.
    I see. So, madam, it was not my nose –

My ugly nose – that was behind our quarrel,
But your fair features. Good.

ROXANE
                              Then there's a favour . . .
How can I tell you? Please, we must go back,
Back to the days when you were like a brother,
In the park, by the lake . . .

CYRANO
                              At Bergerac, of course!
We used to play together every summer.

ROXANE
150 You used to cut the reeds to make your swords.

CYRANO
And you pulled corn-silk for your dollies' hair.

ROXANE
We had such games!

CYRANO
                              Eating green gooseberries . . .

ROXANE
You would do anything I asked you to . . .

CYRANO
Roxane was Madeleine then . . .

ROXANE
                                        Pretty?

CYRANO
                                        Not bad.

ROXANE
Sometimes you'd cut your hand and run to me
And I'd play mother, scolding you and saying,
    [*Taking his hand*]
'How did you do it this time, silly boy?'
    [*Astonished*]
I don't believe it! Bleeding again! What *is* this?
At your age, really! Where did you get this one?

CYRANO
160 I was out playing, near the Porte de Nesle.

ROXANE [*sitting on a table and dipping her handkerchief in a
    glass of water*]

Come, let me see.

CYRANO [*sitting down next to her*]
                    So sweet! So motherly!

ROXANE
How many of them were you fighting this time?

CYRANO
Not quite a hundred.

ROXANE
                        Really! Tell me.

CYRANO
                                    No.
You tell *me* that thing, you know, you were frightened . . .

ROXANE
I'm feeling braver, thinking of the old days.
Well, the thing is, I'm in love.

CYRANO
                            In love. I see.

ROXANE
With someone who doesn't know I love him.

CYRANO
                                            Ah.

ROXANE
I haven't told him yet, but I shall presently.

CYRANO
                                        Ah!

ROXANE
He loves me, but he's shy and daren't speak.

CYRANO
                                        Ah!

ROXANE
Don't take your hand away, it's burning.   170
I'm sure he means to speak to me quite soon.

CYRANO
Indeed!

ROXANE
            And what is most surprising, cousin,
He's in your regiment.

CYRANO
                              Ah!
ROXANE
                              And in your company!
CYRANO
                                             Ah!
ROXANE
  He's proud, brave, noble, handsome . . .
CYRANO [*springing to his feet, turning pale*]
                                    Handsome!
ROXANE
  Why, what's the matter?
CYRANO
                              Nothing, just this hand.
ROXANE
  Anyway, I'm in love. We haven't spoken.
  So far I've only seen him at the theatre.
  But the way he looks at me . . .
CYRANO
                              Can you be sure?
ROXANE
  Out in the evening in the Place Royale
180 Under the trees, the ladies talk, you know.
  One of them dropped a hint.
CYRANO
                              A cadet . . .
ROXANE
                                    In the Guards.
CYRANO
  His name?
ROXANE
              Baron Christian de Neuvillette.
CYRANO
  He's not in the Guards.
ROXANE
                              He joined this morning.

DUENNA [*sticking her head round the door*]
  I've eaten all the pastries, Monsieur Cyrano!
CYRANO [*pushing her out again*]
  Read the bags, then!
CYRANO
                    But Roxane, darling,
  You know how you love poetry, fine language –
  Suppose this boy's a dull, uncultured clod!
ROXANE
  He can't be, look at his hair!
CYRANO
                              His hair! Is that it?
ROXANE
  He simply must be eloquent, I know it!
  He couldn't look like that and be a savage.   190
CYRANO
  Well, handsome does as handsome is, I dare say.
  But if he's stupid . . .
ROXANE
                    Then I'll die, so there!
CYRANO
  You brought me here to tell me that you love him?
  I must admit I cannot see the point.
ROXANE
  Ah, but there is a point. You see, yesterday
  Somebody told me something dreadful. It seems
  That in your company you're all Gascons . . .
CYRANO
  And anyone who isn't, suffers – yes?
ROXANE
  I was so afraid for him.
CYRANO [*muttering to himself*]
                        Rightly!
ROXANE
                              But then I thought –
  When I saw you punish that idiot yesterday,   200
  Facing up to them all – they must be in awe of you,

All of them, so . . .

CYRANO

So, yes, I'll look out for him,
Little de Neuvillette.

ROXANE

Oh, you are good!
I've always been so fond of you, you know.

CYRANO
I know.

ROXANE

You'll really be his friend?

CYRANO

I will.

ROXANE
You'll never let him fight a duel?

CYRANO

Never.

ROXANE
Oh, I do love you! But I must be going . . .
    [*Puts on her mask again. Then, vaguely:*]
The fight last night, it must have been amazing . . .
Tell him to write to me . . .
    [*Blowing a kiss*]

. . . dear Cyrano!

CYRANO
I will.

ROXANE

210   A hundred men! Goodbye, cousin.
Tell him to write. And you must tell me soon
About the fight. A hundred men! Imagine!

CYRANO [*as she leaves*]
It's not the hardest thing I've done today.
    [CYRANO *stands with downcast eyes. A moment's silence,*
    then RAGUENEAU *sticks his head round the door.*]

Scene VII

CYRANO, RAGUENEAU, POETS, CARBON DE CASTEL-
JALOUX, CADETS, CROWD, *then* DE GUICHE

RAGUENEAU
  Can we come in?
CYRANO [*without moving*]
                    Yes.
  [RAGUENEAU *beckons the poets in. At the same time*
  CARBON DE CASTEL-JALOUX, *in the uniform of a captain
  of the Guards, appears at the upstage door, gesturing
  excitedly at the sight of* CYRANO.]
CARBON DE CASTEL-JALOUX
                    Here he is!
CYRANO [*raising his head*]
                          Captain . . .
CARBON [*triumphantly*]
  We know! We've heard it all! Congratulations!
  All the chaps are outside! They want to see you!
CYRANO [*drawing back*]
  But . . .
CARBON [*trying to drag him forward*]
              Come on, you must!
CYRANO
                          No, please . . .
CARBON
  They're just across the road!
CYRANO
                          I'd really rather . . .
CARBON [*returns to the door and calls loudly to the cadets
    offstage*]
  He doesn't want to talk, he's out of sorts!
VOICES [*offstage*]
  Ridiculous! Absurd! We're coming!
  [*Noise offstage, clinking of swords, boots approaching.*]

CARBON [*rubbing his hands*]

220   Good!

CADETS [*bursting on to the stage*]
Od's death! Od's life! Od's blood! Od's bodikins!

RAGUENEAU [*timidly*]
Are you all Gascons, gentlemen?

CADETS
                                        That's right!

A CADET
Well done, Cyrano!

CYRANO
                          Baron . . .

ANOTHER [*shaking both of* CYRANO'*s hands*]
                                        Good man!

CYRANO
                                                Baron . . .

A THIRD
Let's give him a hug!
[*All crowd around him.*]

CYRANO
                          Baron . . . Baron . . . please . . .

RAGUENEAU
All barons too?

CADETS
                    All of us!

RAGUENEAU [*to* CYRANO, *aside*]
                              Are they really?

FIRST CADET
Our coronets would stretch from here to doomsday!
[*Enter* LE BRET, *running towards* CYRANO.]

LE BRET
Everyone wants to see you. There's a crowd.

CYRANO [*horrified*]
You didn't tell them where I was . . .

LE BRET [*complacently*]
                                        Of course!

A BOURGEOIS
Sir, my respects. The whole Marais is here!

[*Through the door a crowd can be seen in the street, with carriages and sedan chairs.*]

LE BRET [*aside to* CYRANO, *smiling*]
  What happened with Roxane?

CYRANO [*anguished*]

                                Please . . .

CROWD [*outside*]

                                Cyrano!   230

  We want Cyrano! Let us in!
  [*They burst into the shop, pushing and shoving. Cheers.*]

RAGUENEAU

                                My shop!
  They're breaking everything! It's wonderful!

PEOPLE [*around* CYRANO]
  Cyrano, old man . . . Cyrano, my dear friend . . .

CYRANO
  I never had so many friends before.

LE BRET [*delighted*]
  That's success!

A MARQUIS [*running towards* CYRANO, *his hands outstretched*]
                                Dear boy, if you'd only seen . . .

CYRANO [*icily*]
  Have we met before?

ANOTHER

                                Sir, may I introduce you . . .
  Some ladies long to meet you . . .

CYRANO [*ditto*]

                                Why, of course,
  If someone introduces you to me.

LE BRET [*amazed*]
  What are you doing?

CYRANO

                                Quiet!

A MAN OF LETTERS [*with a notebook*]
                                Have you a moment?

CYRANO
  No.

LE BRET [*nudging him*]

240   That's Théophraste Renaudot.
He's started a Gazette.

CYRANO

                              What's that to me?

LE BRET

It's full of all the very latest news:
They say the notion really might catch on.

A POET [*coming forward*]

Sir, if I may . . .

CYRANO

                    What now?

POET

                              I mean to write
A quintuple acrostic on your name . . .

SOMEONE ELSE

Sir!

CYRANO

   That's enough.
[*Noise outside. A path is cleared and* LE BRET *appears in
the doorway with an escort including* CUIGY, BRISSAILLE
and the officers who left the stage with CYRANO *at the end
of Act I.* CUIGY *rushes up to* CYRANO.]

CUIGY

                    Monsieur de Guiche has come
[*Awed murmur from the crowd*]
Bringing a message from the Maréchal.
Our noble Maréchal de Gassion
Sends you his compliment on last night's exploit.

CYRANO [*bowing*]

250   The Maréchal's a man of courage. I thank him.

DE GUICHE

He would have found the tale beyond belief
Had not these gentlemen been there to see it.

CUIGY

With our own eyes!

LE BRET [*aside, to* CYRANO, *who does not seem to be listening*]

What's the matter?

CYRANO

Quiet!

LE BRET
You look sad.

CYRANO

What! In front of all these people?
[*He draws himself up, puffs out his chest: his moustache bristles.*]

DE GUICHE
It seems you've made yourself a name already
For feats of daring. You're a Gascon, aren't you?

CYRANO
A cadet, yes.

A CADET [*fiercely*]

One of us.

DE GUICHE

Ah, I see.
All of those fearsome-looking gentlemen
Are the famous ...

CARBON

Cyrano!

CYRANO

Yes, captain?

CARBON
We're all present, I think. Will you do the honours?   260

CYRANO [*taking two steps towards* DE GUICHE *and gesturing towards the cadets*]
We are the boys from Gascony,
Captain Carbon's cadets.
Fighters and swaggerers born to be,
Each of us has a family tree
Lost in the mists of antiquity.
Laden with glory and debts,

We are the boys from Gascony
Captain Carbon's cadets.

With an eagle's eye and a walk so proud,
270   Tiger's moustache and a wolfish grin,
Holes in our hats but our heads unbowed,
We cut our way through the muttering crowd.
When they call us shabby we laugh aloud
And wait for the fun to begin,
With an eagle's eye and a walk so proud
And a sinister wolfish grin.

Here come the boys from Gascony,
Husbands, expect the worst!
Come along, ladies, don't be shy,
280   We bring our mettle for you to try.
We'll go to the fighting by and by –
Our duties to you come first!
Here come the boys from Gascony
Husbands, expect the worst!

Southern savages, imps of hell
Are our usual epithets.
Every house has a tale to tell
Of the distant fields where our fathers fell,
But southern savages, hell-hounds – well,
290   That's as polite as it gets.
And savages, imps or hounds of hell,
We're Captain Carbon's cadets.

DE GUICHE
   It's quite the thing now to support a poet –
   Will you accept my patronage?
CYRANO
                              No, no one's.
DE GUICHE
   Your spirit was remarkable last night;
   My uncle Richelieu remarked on it.
   Shall I present you to him?

LE BRET
                              What a chance!
DE GUICHE
  No doubt you have some manuscripts to show him.
LE BRET
  Your *Agrippina*! You can have it staged!
DE GUICHE
  Take it along.
CYRANO [*almost tempted*]
                            Perhaps . . .
DE GUICHE
                                    He's quite an expert.   300
  He'll make the odd correction here and there . . .
CYRANO
  No, that's impossible: my blood runs cold
  To think of someone else touching a word.
DE GUICHE
  But when he finds a line he likes, he's generous.
CYRANO
  Not generous enough: I'll be the judge.
  Meeting my standards is my own reward.
DE GUICHE
  You're very proud.
CYRANO
                          You've noticed.
  [*Enter a* CADET. *On his sword are threaded several
  battered hats with broken feathers.*]
CADET
                                    Cyrano,
  Look what we found just now on the embankment.
  Have you seen feathered game like this before?
  The cowards ran away and left their hats!   310
CARBON
  To the victors the spoils!
    [*All laugh.*]
CUIGY
                              Their master must be raging.
  Who can have sent them?

DE GUICHE
                              I did. They were sent
To make a drunken rhymester pay the price.
A gentleman can't do these things himself.
    [*An embarrassed silence.*]
CADET [*showing the hats to* CYRANO]
    What can we make of them? They're full of grease.
    Rillettes, perhaps?
CYRANO [*taking the sword and sliding the hats down it, so
    that they land at* DE GUICHE'*s feet*]
                        Monsieur de Guiche, I think
    These things belong to you, or to your friends?
DE GUICHE
    My chair and porters, quickly. Tell me, sir . . .
VOICE IN THE STREET
    Chair for Monsieur de Guiche!
DE GUICHE
320 Have you ever read the tale of *Don Quixote*?
CYRANO
    I've great respect for that eccentric knight.
DE GUICHE
    I recommend the chapter on the windmills.
CYRANO
    Chapter thirteen.
PORTER [*appearing at the door*]
                        Your chair, my lord.
DE GUICHE
                                    Remember:
    Tilting at windmills is a dangerous game.
CYRANO
    My enemies will turn with every breeze?
DE GUICHE
    When the great sails come round, they'll strike you down
    Into the mud.
CYRANO
                Or lift me to the stars.
    [*Exit* DE GUICHE. LE BRET *formally accompanies him to
    the door and we see him getting into his sedan chair. The*

*gentlemen leave, whispering to each other, and the crowd
disperses.* CYRANO, CADETS *and* LE BRET *sit at the tables
and prepare to eat.*]

Scene VIII

CYRANO, LE BRET, CADETS

CYRANO [*cheerfully waving to the crowd as they slink away,
    not daring to say goodbye*]
  Goodbye, gentlemen, it was a pleasure . . .
LE BRET
                                            Now
  Look what you've done!
CYRANO
                          Well?
LE BRET
                                Why must you always
  Throw people's kindness back in their faces?
CYRANO
                                              Kindness!   330
LE BRET
  If you could only swallow your pride.
CYRANO
                                        And do what?
  Find a protector, I suppose, a patron,
  And cling to him like ivy round a tree?
  Pull myself up by sticking to his bark?
  Thank you, but no. Write fulsome dedications
  To money-men, as other poets do?
  Play the buffoon and hope to bring a smile
  To politicians' lips? Thank you, but no.
  Swallow a toad each day, crawl on my belly,
  Wear out my breeches at the knees, bend double   340
  In all directions – no thanks. Butter up fools,
  Become the poet of a ladies' circle,

Their very own tame genius – I don't think so.
Pay the *right* publisher to print my poems?[1]
Thank you, but no. Lay down the law in cafés,
Base a whole reputation on one poem
Instead of writing more? Thanks, but no thanks.
Idolize idiots, live in fear of the press,
Wake every day and think, 'What are they saying
350   About me this morning?' No, that's not for me.
Laying my plans, living in fear and trembling,
Visiting 'useful' people instead of writing,
Signing petitions, angling for introductions . . .
No, no, no! I can't live like that!
I want to lead my life, to be free, to dream,
To open my eyes to the world and write what I see;
To set my hat at the angle I want to wear it
And, if anyone doesn't like it, fight if I choose,
Never having to think of fame or money,
360   Just work. I'll send my hero to the moon
If I think fit. All that I write is mine
And that's the way I want it to stay. Perhaps
It isn't much, but it's my own, and if
By chance I do have some success, why then
That will be mine as well – no one to thank.
I'm not a parasite, to cling and climb:
I may not be an oak tree, but by heaven
I swear I'll rise alone or not at all.

LE BRET
    All right, without your friends, but not *against* them!
370   Why do you have this love of picking quarrels
    And making enemies everywhere you go?

CYRANO
    It's seeing you make friends at every turn!
    When you go down the street they all appear
    Simpering with puckered mouths like a chicken's bum!
    Rather than have them smile at me like that
    I say, 'Another enemy! Hurrah!'

LE BRET
    Absurd!

CYRANO
   I like annoying people, I admit it.
A man stands straighter under hostile eyes.
My doublet's well adorned with envious spittle
And cowards' drool. Your easy kind of friendship   380
Is like the linen men wear nowadays,
Those floppy lace affairs that let you slouch
Italian fashion. But my Spanish ruff
Is starched and boned by hatred every day.
I have to hold my head up when I wear it
And each new enemy's another layer
That braces me for torture and for glory.
  [*A pause.*]   390
LE BRET [*quietly, taking* CYRANO's *arm*]
Very impressive speech, my friend, but now
Why don't you just admit she doesn't love you?
  [CHRISTIAN *has entered and approached the cadets, but*
  they do not speak to him and he eventually sits at a small
  table by himself.]

Scene IX

  CYRANO, LE BRET, CADETS, CHRISTIAN DE NEU-
  VILLETTE

A CADET [*sitting at a table with a glass in his hand*]
Hey, Cyrano!
  [CYRANO *turns round.*]
    Tell us what happened.
CYRANO
           Later.   400
  [*He goes on talking to* LE BRET.]
CADET [*rising and walking to* CHRISTIAN's *table*]
The fight! Go on, tell the new boy.
CHRISTIAN
        New boy?

ANOTHER CADET

That's right, northerner! Wet behind the ears!

CHRISTIAN

Wet, am I?

FIRST CADET [*teasing*]

Listen, Monsieur de Neuvillette:

In this place there's one thing we never mention.

CHRISTIAN

And that is . . .

ANOTHER CADET [*touching his nose three times, with a mysterious look*]

Look! Now do you understand?

CHRISTIAN

I see, it's . . .

ALL

Shh!

ANOTHER CADET

Nobody says that word,

[*Pointing to* CYRANO]

Or *he*'s the one they have to answer to.

ANOTHER [*who has crept up behind the first*]

Two chaps with colds, he ran them through one day:

He said that they were talking through their . . . [*Taps
nose.*]

ANOTHER [*crawling out from under the table, in a sepulchral
voice*]

410   To mention things olfactory entitles

The rash one to a rapier through his vitals!

ANOTHER

You only have to say the word – to say it?

The merest hint's enough, the smallest gesture –

Reach for your handkerchief and reach for death!

[*Silence. All the cadets surround* CHRISTIAN, *looking at
him with their arms folded. He goes to* CARBON *who is
talking to another officer and pretending not to hear the
cadets.*]

CHRISTIAN

Captain . . .

CARBON [*looking him up and down*]
            Yes?
CHRISTIAN
                  What does a person do
  When southerners boast too much?
CARBON
                              Why, then of course
  He shows them northerners can stand their ground.
    [*Turns his back.*]
CHRISTIAN
  Thank you.
FIRST CADET [*to* CYRANO]
                  Now, the story!
CYRANO
                        The story?
ALL
                              The story!
    [CYRANO *comes downstage to the cadets, who draw their
    stools up to listen.* CHRISTIAN *sits a slight distance away,
    straddling a chair.*]
CYRANO
  Well, I was marching out to meet the foe.
  The moon was shining like a silver watch,   420
  When suddenly a heavenly jeweller's hand
  Took up a cotton cloud and passed it over
  Her polished face, and in that very instant
  The night became as black as pitch. You know
  There are no street-lamps by the Seine, and so
  A man could see no further . . .
CHRISTIAN
                        Than the end of his nose.
    [*All rise to their feet, looking at* CYRANO *in terror.*
    CYRANO *has stopped speaking, astonished. Pause.*]
CYRANO
  Who is that man?
A CADET [*timidly*]
                  He's new sir, came today,

CYRANO [*moving towards* CHRISTIAN]
Today?
CARBON [*in an undertone*]
          He's the Baron de Neuvillette.
CYRANO [*stopping in his tracks*]
   Ah, I see.
          [*Turns pale, reddens again, moves towards* CHRISTIAN,
          then stops again. Continues in a carefully controlled voice:]
               Very well. As I was saying . . .
          [*furiously*] God damn it!

430   [*controlled*] It was dark, I couldn't see,
   Still I walked forward, saying to myself
   That now, by siding with a nobody
   I'd picked a quarrel with a powerful man
   And run the risk of getting . . .
CHRISTIAN
                                   Up his nose.
          [*All rise again, except* CHRISTIAN *who sits swinging on
          his chair.*]
CYRANO [*almost choking*]
   On the wrong side of him. I'd stuck . . .
CHRISTIAN
                                   My nose . . .
CYRANO
   My fingers into someone else's business
   And now he'd want to hit me . . .
CHRISTIAN
                                   On the nose . . .
CYRANO [*wiping his brow*]
   As hard as he could. But there, I said to myself,
   A Gascon never retreats. Forward I charged!
   Into the dark, and something struck . . .
CHRISTIAN
440   My nose . . .
CYRANO
   God damn it!
          [*He springs towards* CHRISTIAN. *All the Gascons rush*

*forward to see, but as he reaches him he regains control
and continues his story.*]
                    I returned the blow, and there . . .
CHRISTIAN
  Under my nose . . .
CYRANO
                            A hundred drunken brawlers . . .
CHRISTIAN
  Stinking to heaven . . .
CYRANO [*pale, trying to force a smile*]
                            Of garlic. I lowered my head . . .
CHRISTIAN
  Followed my nose . . .
CYRANO
                        And charged! One I impaled,
  Two I ran through the body – so – until
  The others cried, 'It's him . . .'
CHRISTIAN
                            The conkering hero!
CYRANO [*exploding*]
  Right! That's it! Out!
  [*Cadets scuttle for the door.*]
FIRST CADET
                    Now he's done it!
CYRANO
  All of you! Out! Leave me alone with this man.
SECOND CADET
  When we get back we'll find him chopped in pieces!
RAGUENEAU
  Mincemeat!
ANOTHER CADET
            For one of your pies!
RAGUENEAU
                            I feel quite weak!   450
CADET
  I can't bear to think of it!
ANOTHER
                    Nor can I!

[*All make their escape, by the wings, stairs or door.* CHRISTIAN *and* CYRANO *look at each other. A pause.*]

Scene X

CYRANO, CHRISTIAN

CYRANO

                 Come here.

CHRISTIAN
  Sir?

CYRANO
    You're brave.

CHRISTIAN

          Thank you.

CYRANO

            Very brave.
  It's better that way.

CHRISTIAN

        May I ask . . . ?

CYRANO

              Come here.
  Give me a hug. I'm her brother.

CHRISTIAN

            Whose brother?

CYRANO
  Hers.

CHRISTIAN
    But whose?

CYRANO

        Roxane's, of course.

CHRISTIAN

            Her brother!

CYRANO
  Well, near enough: her cousin.

CHRISTIAN
                              Did she tell you . . . ?
CYRANO
  Everything.
CHRISTIAN
                         Does she love me?
CYRANO
                                    What do you think?
CHRISTIAN [*taking both* CYRANO'*s hands in his*]
  I'm so glad to meet you!
CYRANO
                              You could have fooled me!
CHRISTIAN
  I'm sorry.
CYRANO [*putting his hand on* CHRISTIAN'*s shoulder*]
                    Yes, the boy is handsome, damn him!
CHRISTIAN
  Believe me, sir, I really do admire you.   460
CYRANO
  What, nose and all?
CHRISTIAN
                         I was a fool.
CYRANO
                                    Now listen.
  Roxane expects to hear from you tonight.
CHRISTIAN
  So much the worse for me.
CYRANO
                              What do you mean?
CHRISTIAN
  If once I speak to her, it's over.
CYRANO
                                    Why?
CHRISTIAN
  I'm just so stupid, I could die of shame.
CYRANO
  No, you're not stupid if you think you are.

And anyhow, the way you went for me –
That wasn't stupid, was it?

CHRISTIAN

                              Oh, that's different.
I can attack with words, that's what a man does.
470 But then with women, all my words dry up.
I see them looking at me as I pass . . .

CYRANO

But when you stop and talk . . .

CHRISTIAN

                                        That's what I dread:
All those long conversations about love.

CYRANO

I've often thought that with a better profile
I could have done that kind of thing quite well.

CHRISTIAN

Oh, for the words to speak my thoughts with grace!

CYRANO [aside]

Oh, the advantage of a pretty face!

CHRISTIAN

She's used to eloquence: she'll laugh at me.

CYRANO [suddenly]

Not if you use my words. Together we
480 Can make the perfect man: your looks, my voice.

CHRISTIAN

What?

CYRANO

            If I write your lines for you every day,
Can you learn them?

CHRISTIAN

                              I'm sorry . . .

CYRANO

                                        Think, man!
You didn't want to disappoint Roxane . . .
Well, if we work together, she'll be happy.
Under this leather jerkin there's a heart:
Let's slip it under your embroidered coat.
What do you say?

CHRISTIAN
                     Cyrano, are you sure?
The thought frightens me.
CYRANO
                             Come on, we can do it.
My words on your lips.
CHRISTIAN
                        Look at your eyes, they're shining.
Do you really want to?
CYRANO [*his eyes gleaming for a moment*]
                       Well, it would be fun.   490
   [*Adopting an offhand manner*]
A scheme like that is bound to tempt an artist:
I complete you, you complete me – perfection.
You'll be in sunlight, I'll be in the shadows.
I'll be your inspiration, you my beauty.
CHRISTIAN
But I need the letter now, what can I do?
CYRANO [*producing from his pocket the letter he wrote
    earlier*]
Here's a letter, ready to order.
CHRISTIAN
                      How did you . . . ?
CYRANO
All complete, just the address to add.
CHRISTIAN
I can't . . .
CYRANO
             Yes, you can. Go on, it's a good one.
CHRISTIAN
But how did you manage . . .
CYRANO
                 Oh, you know, we poets
Always have letters about us, all invented,   500
Written to Chloris, Phyllis[1] and so on . . .
Dreams wrapped in a name . . . Take it, dear boy,
And turn my idle dreams to flesh and blood.
All of my protestations, made to thin air,

Will settle on the branches of your love.
[*A pause.*]
The words are eloquent, I do admit –
All the more so for being insincere –
Go on, take it, please . . .
CHRISTIAN
                              Will it do for me?
Won't there be certain things we'll have to change?
CYRANO
510   It'll be perfect. Women are so vain
She'll think each word was written just for her.
CHRISTIAN [*throwing his arms round* CYRANO]
     You're a real friend.

Scene XI

CYRANO, CHRISTIAN, GASCONS, MUSKETEER, LISE

[*A* CADET *looks gingerly round the door.*]
CADET
                         Nothing. A deathly hush . . .
I daren't look. [*Puts his head further in.*]
                         What! I don't believe it!
[*The other cadets follow him in and are dumbfounded to
see* CYRANO *and* CHRISTIAN *with their arms around each
other.*]
MUSKETEER
     Well! Aren't they sweet!
CARBON
                         The wolf's become a lamb.
Who would have thought he'd turn the other . . . nostril?
MUSKETEER
     So we can talk about his nose now, can we?
Hey, Lise! Come and see this!
     [*Loudly*]
                              I think I smell

Something peculiar.
  [*Goes to* CYRANO, *stares at his nose.*]
                    Can you smell it, sir?
  [*Sniffs ostentatiously.*]
I wonder now, what can it be?
CYRANO [*boxing his ears*]
                         It's pigshit!
  [*Delight among the cadets: their old* CYRANO *is back.
  Somersaults, horseplay.*]

ACT III

ROXANE'S KISS

Scene: a little square in the old Marais, surrounded by venerable houses. Stage L, ROXANE's house, with a tree overhanging its garden wall. Over the door a window and balcony. A bench outside the door.

Ivy on the walls, jasmine around and hanging down from the balcony. The bench and the irregular stone of the wall give footholds to climb up to the window.

Stage R, another old house of the same kind, brick with stone dressings, the main entrance visible. The door-knocker is bandaged up like a sore thumb.

DUENNA is discovered sitting on the bench. ROXANE's window is wide open to her balcony. Next to DUENNA is RAGUENEAU dressed in a kind of servant's livery, finishing a story and wiping his eyes.

Scene I

RAGUENEAU, DUENNA, *then* ROXANE, CYRANO *and two* PAGES

RAGUENEAU
  . . . And then she left me for a musketeer.
  I thought I'd hang myself, all on my own,
  Without a penny, what could I do? But then
  Monsieur de Bergerac came and cut me down
  And gave me to his cousin as her steward.

DUENNA
  But why without a penny?
RAGUENEAU
                            Well, you see,
  Lise had a taste for soldiers, I for poets:
  The crumbs that were let fall by Phoebus' children
  Were polished off by Mars, and that was that.
DUENNA
  Roxane, dear, are you ready? They're expecting us.   10
ROXANE [*indoors*]
  Just putting on my cloak.
DUENNA
                            Across the road,
  That's where we're both invited, to Clomire's.
  Her circle meets there every week: today
  A gentleman is going to talk on Love.
RAGUENEAU
  Love, you say?
DUENNA
                  Exactly.
    [*Calling up to the window*]
                            Hurry, Roxane,
  Or else we'll miss that interesting talk!
ROXANE
  Coming!
    [CYRANO's *voice is heard in the wings, accompanied by
    musicians.*]
DUENNA
                  Now what is this, a serenade?
    [*Enter* CYRANO *with two pages playing theorbos.*[1]]
CYRANO
  A demisemiquaver, stupid boy!
A PAGE [*sarcastically*]
  A demisemiquaver! You're an expert
  I see, sir!
CYRANO
              Yes, that's it, an expert.   20
  All of Gassendi's[2] pupils are musicians.

[*He takes the theorbo and plays a flourish on it.* ROXANE
appears on the balcony.]

ROXANE

Is that you?

CYRANO [*singing*]

Madam, 'tis I, your slave

Come to adore your lilies and your roses.

ROXANE

Wait a minute.

DUENNA

Who are those clever children?

CYRANO

I won them from d'Assoucy: we were arguing

About a point of grammar, and he bet me

A whole day's music. Well, he lost, of course.

And so, till Phoebus' car remounts the skies

These dainty boys will follow in my footsteps

30   Accompanying every move I make

With sweet, melodious sounds. The trouble is,

I'm starting to get tired of it already.

Run along, children, now: why don't you go

And offer Montfleury a serenade

From me. A lovely long one – out of tune.

[*As they leave, to* DUENNA]

Duenna, dear, I've come to ask Roxane –

As I do every evening – if the man

She loves is still as perfect as she thinks him.

ROXANE [*coming out of the house*]

He is – perfect – so handsome – and I love him.

CYRANO

So clever too?

ROXANE

40   Cleverer even than you.

CYRANO

If you say so.

ROXANE

I do! I love the way

He turns sweet nothings into perfect form.

Sometimes he seems to fail, the Muse deserts him,
But then he'll think of something just divine.
   [DUENNA *goes into the house.*]

CYRANO
   Really.

ROXANE
               Oh, that's just so like you men.
   You think a handsome person can't be clever.

CYRANO
   No doubt he likes to talk about his feelings.

ROXANE
   Talk! He's a poet!

CYRANO
                      And he writes, you say.

ROXANE
   Listen to what he sent me yesterday:
   My heart is yours, yet in my bosom swells . . .   50
      [CYRANO *pulls a face.*]

ROXANE
   What about this, then: *Heartless, who can pine?*
   Give me my heart again, though it be thine.

CYRANO
   First he's got too much heart, then not enough.
   How can he hope to win you with such stuff?

ROXANE
   Very amusing. Anyone can see
   You're jealous.

CYRANO
               Jealous!

ROXANE
                      Of his talent.

CYRANO
                                   Me!

ROXANE
   Listen to this, though: *All my heart's one ache:*
   If kisses could be written down on paper
   You'd have to read this letter with your lips.

CYRANO [*smiling in spite of himself*]
    That's not too bad . . .
        [*sternly*]
60   . . . but very sentimental.
ROXANE
    And this . . .
CYRANO [*delighted*]
                Do you know all his letters off by heart?
ROXANE
    Every last one.
CYRANO [*curling his moustache*]
                How flattering!
ROXANE
                            He's a genius.
CYRANO [*modestly*]
    A genius! Hardly . . .
ROXANE [*determined*]
                    Yes, I said a genius.
CYRANO [*giving way gracefully*]
    If you insist, a genius.
        [*Re-enter* DUENNA, *flustered.*]
DUENNA
                    Monsieur de Guiche!
    Come inside, sir. Don't let him see you here.
ROXANE
    He might suspect the secret of my heart!
    He loves me too; he has the power to harm me.
    He mustn't know!
CYRANO
                All right, I'm going in.
        [CYRANO *goes into the house. Enter* DE GUICHE.]

Scene II

ROXANE, DE GUICHE, DUENNA *at a distance*

ROXANE [*curtsying to* DE GUICHE]
  You'll excuse me sir, I was just leaving.
DE GUICHE
  I came to say goodbye.
ROXANE
                    You're leaving too?   70
DE GUICHE
  For the war.
ROXANE
            Ah!
DE GUICHE
              Tonight.
ROXANE
                    Ah! Indeed!
DE GUICHE
  I have the orders: we besiege Arras.[1]
ROXANE
  Besiege Arras . . .
DE GUICHE
              You hardly seem bereft.
  I, on the contrary, am broken-hearted
  To leave you here alone. When shall I see you?
  You know I am the officer commanding
  The regiment of Guards.
ROXANE [*alarmed*]
                    The Guards?
DE GUICHE
  Yes, where your cousin serves, that brawling boaster –
  I shall enjoy finding a place for *him*.
ROXANE
  Are the Guards going to battle?

DE GUICHE [*laughing*]

80   Well, of course.

They are my regiment.

ROXANE [*aside, almost choking*]

                                   Christian!

DE GUICHE

                                        What's the matter?

ROXANE

The thought of war ... someone one knows ...

DE GUICHE

                                               Dear child!

    [*Aside, touched*]

The first sign ever that she cares for me!

ROXANE

Now let me see – revenge against my cousin ...

DE GUICHE

You're on his side?

ROXANE

                         Why no, I hardly see him.

DE GUICHE

He's always seen around with that cadet,

What is his name – Neuville –

ROXANE

                                   The tall one?

DE GUICHE

                                           Fair.

ROXANE

Reddish.

DE GUICHE

        And handsome.

ROXANE

                         Hmm ...

DE GUICHE

                                   But an idiot.

ROXANE

I'd say so.

    [*Changing to a businesslike tone*]

        Now, your revenge on Cyrano.

Why give him a chance to make his name? 90
Fighting is what he loves, don't let him do it.
I've got a better plan: leave him at home.
Him and his precious cadets, sitting in Paris,
Twiddling their thumbs when the army goes to war.
He'll eat his heart out!

DE GUICHE

Wonderful! Just like a woman!
Trust a woman to think of a real revenge!
  [*Sentimentally*]
You do love me a little after all?
I see you *can* feel love for a man.

ROXANE

Perhaps.

DE GUICHE [*showing a packet of papers*]
These are the orders: every company
Will have them today – apart from the cadets! 100
Theirs I'll keep: imagine Cyrano's face!
Are you always so wicked, tell me?

ROXANE [*sweetly*]

What do you mean?

DE GUICHE
Listen, I *am* supposed to leave this evening,
But how can I leave you now . . . In a street nearby
There's a monastery – holy men – no laymen admitted –
I could hide there till dusk. My uncle's been good to them.
I'll come to you masked. Let me have one more day!

ROXANE
But if you're missed, your reputation . . .

DE GUICHE

Bah!

ROXANE
Arras . . . the siege . . .

DE GUICHE

It can wait a day.
  [*Making to kiss her*]

Dear girl!

ROXANE
   No!
DE GUICHE
   I must!
ROXANE
              You know I can't. Now go!
   [*Aside*] And Christian stays! [*Aloud*] Farewell, Antoine,
      brave heart!
DE GUICHE
   She called me by my name! You *are* in love, then . . .
ROXANE
   Love for the man I feared for.
DE GUICHE
                     Blessed word!
   Now I can leave without a qualm. Goodbye!
      [*Anxious afterthought*]
   I'm not presuming . . .
ROXANE
              No, dear friend.
DE GUICHE
                       Adieu!
               [*Exit* DE GUICHE.]
DUENNA [*curtsying to his retreating back, parodying*
   ROXANE's *tone*]
   No, dear friend. Adieu!
ROXANE
             Now not a word
   To Cyrano of what I've done – he'd never
   Forgive me for denying him his war.
   Cousin!

Scene III

ROXANE, DUENNA, CYRANO

ROXANE [*to* CYRANO, *as he comes out of the house*]
    We're going to Clomire's.
    [*Points to the door across the way.*]
                           Alcandre's coming,
And Lysimon.
DUENNA
                  Yes, but a little bird   120
Tells me we'll be too late.
CYRANO
                  Oh, that won't do.
You mustn't miss the circus.
DUENNA
                Look at that!
The knocker's all wrapped up.
    [*To the knocker*]
                  See there, they've gagged you,
You naughty boy, to stop you interrupting
During the conversation.
    [*She knocks quietly, with infinite precautions. The door is
    opened.*]
ROXANE
                Let's go in.
    [*To* CYRANO]
If Christian comes, as I expect he will,
Ask him to wait.
CYRANO
          And what's the subject, please,
Of today's examination?
ROXANE
            You won't tell?
CYRANO
    No.

ROXANE
        There's no fixed subject. 'Talk,' I shall say.
130   Just improvise on love – magnificently.
CYRANO
        I see.
ROXANE
        Don't tell.
CYRANO
                                    I promise.
        [*As she disappears through the door*]
                                    Thanks for the tip!
        [ROXANE *pokes her head out again.*]
ROXANE
        He'd practise beforehand!
CYRANO
                                    Surely not!
        [*Once she is gone*]
                                    Christian!

Scene IV

CYRANO, CHRISTIAN

CYRANO [*hastily, to* CHRISTIAN]
        Here it all is, ready to learn by heart.
        This is your chance to make a real impression.
        Quick, let's get started. Oh, don't look so glum.
        Let's go to your place, I can teach you . . .
CHRISTIAN
                                            No.
CYRANO
                                            What?
CHRISTIAN
        I'd rather not. I'll wait for Roxane here.

CYRANO
  Are you insane? Quick, let me show you . . .
CHRISTIAN
                                        No.
  I'm tired of using someone else's letters,
  Delivering your speeches, playing a part,   140
  Always afraid of being found out!
  It was all right to start with, but now she loves me,
  I'm sure she does. Thanks, Cyrano, but now
  I can speak for myself.
CYRANO
                      I see.
CHRISTIAN
                                    Anyway,
  How do you know I won't be able to do it?
  I'm not a complete fool. Just wait and see.
  I've learnt a lot from you, and I'm grateful for that.
  But now let me do it myself. If all else fails
  I can always kiss her, can't I?
      [Seeing ROXANE coming out of Clomire's house]
                              Help, it's her!
  Cyrano, don't leave me!
CYRANO
                          You're on your own.   150

                            Scene V

CHRISTIAN, ROXANE, *PRÉCIEUX*, *PRÉCIEUSES* and for
a moment, DUENNA. ROXANE *bidding goodbye to the*
company. Bows and kisses.

PRÉCIEUSES
  Barthénoïde! . . . Alcandre! Grémione!
DUENNA
  Oh, it's too bad! We missed the Land of Love![1]

ROXANE [*still bidding goodbye*]
  Urimédonte! . . . Goodbye!
    [*All say goodbye to* ROXANE, *and again to each other,
    then separate and head for home in different directions.*
    ROXANE *sees* CHRISTIAN.]
                          Why, it's you! [*Going to him*]
      Don't go.
  They're leaving, and it's such a lovely evening.
  Shall we sit and enjoy the air? It's quiet now,
  No one about, and you can talk to me.
CHRISTIAN [*sits beside her on the bench. A long pause, then*]
  I love you.
ROXANE [*closing her eyes*]
          That's right. Talk to me of love.
CHRISTIAN
  I love you.
ROXANE
        So you said. Elaborate.
CHRISTIAN
  I said I love . . .
ROXANE
            Expand, I said! Develop!
CHRISTIAN
  I love you so much.
ROXANE
160   Yes, you love me, and . . . ?
CHRISTIAN
  And . . . I'd be so happy if *you* loved *me*.
  Do you, Roxane? Do you love me too?
ROXANE [*irritated*]
  Is this the cream of your eloquence? More like skim!
  Explain to me just how you love me.
CHRISTIAN
                          So much!
ROXANE
  Unfold your feelings, man, anatomize them!

CHRISTIAN [*who has been staring at the nape of her neck*]
  Your neck! Oh, dearest, let me kiss it!
ROXANE
                                Christian!
CHRISTIAN
  I love you!
ROXANE [*making to rise*]
           Not again!
CHRISTIAN [*desperately, restraining her*]
               No, I don't love you.
ROXANE [*sitting down again*]
  That's better.
CHRISTIAN
           I adore you.
ROXANE [*moving away again*]
                This is silly!
CHRISTIAN
  It's making me stupid.
ROXANE
              Well, you said it.
  And I don't like you stupid, any more   170
  Than I'd like you ugly.
CHRISTIAN
              Only let me try . . .
ROXANE
  Go home and try to get your wits together.
CHRISTIAN
  I . . .
ROXANE
    You love me, I know, you said so. Now goodbye.
  [*She goes towards the house.*]
CHRISTIAN
  Don't go, please wait, I need to tell you . . .
ROXANE [*opening the front door*]
                         What?
  That you adore me? Thanks. Goodnight.
  [*Goes in and shuts the door.*]

CYRANO [*who has been on stage for a few moments, unnoticed*]

Well done!

Scene VI

CHRISTIAN, CYRANO *and briefly the* PAGES

CHRISTIAN
  Help me!
CYRANO
        Sorry!
CHRISTIAN
            If I can't get her back
  I'll die, I swear . . .
CYRANO
                And what am I to do?
  Teach you, in five minutes . . . ?
CHRISTIAN
                    Oh look, there she is!
  [*A light appears in the balcony window.*]
CYRANO [*touched*]
  Her window!
CHRISTIAN [*loudly*]
            I shall die!
CYRANO
                Quiet!
CHRISTIAN [*in a whisper*]
                Die!
CYRANO
  It's pitch dark . . .
CHRISTIAN
            Well, then?
CYRANO
                There's just a chance . . .
180
  Not that you deserve . . . Stand there, you idiot!

There, by the balcony. I'll stand underneath
And prompt you.
CHRISTIAN
                         But . . .
CYRANO
                                  No buts!
PAGES [*reappearing upstage*]
                                       Hey, Cyrano!
CYRANO
   Quiet!
FIRST PAGE [*sotto voce*]
              We serenaded Montfleury and . . .
CYRANO [*hurriedly*]
   Go and keep watch at both ends of the street,
   And if there's any sign of someone coming
   Play a tune.
SECOND PAGE
                 What tune, philosopher?
CYRANO
   Sad for a woman, cheerful for a man.
                   [*Exeunt the pages, in opposite directions.*]
   Now call her back!
CHRISTIAN
                        Roxane!
CYRANO
                             Wait! Throw some pebbles.
   [*He throws some pebbles at the window.*]

Scene VII

ROXANE, CHRISTIAN, CYRANO *under the balcony*

ROXANE [*half opening her window*]
   Who calls my name?
CHRISTIAN
                      Me.

ROXANE

                              Me?

CHRISTIAN

190   Christian.

ROXANE [*disdainfully*]
    Oh, you.

CHRISTIAN
          I need to talk to you.

CYRANO

                              Good!
    That's the way, almost a whisper.

ROXANE

                              No!
    You've nothing to say. Go away!

CHRISTIAN

                              Please!

ROXANE

                              No!
    I don't believe you love me.

CHRISTIAN [*prompted by* CYRANO]
                              Gods above!
    Not love you, when 'tis plain I die of love!

ROXANE [*on the point of closing the window, changing her
    mind*]

                              That's better.

CHRISTIAN [*still prompted*]
    Rocked in the cradle of my anxious heart
    The cruel infant hones his playful dart.

ROXANE

                              Much better!
    But if you fear him, sir, were it not best
    E'en now to stifle him within the nest?

CHRISTIAN

200   Alas, such work's too hard for hands like these:
    The smiling babe's an infant Hercules.[1]

ROXANE

                              Excellent!

CHRISTIAN
  As they approached his cradle, he reached out
  And strangled both those serpents, Pride and Doubt.
ROXANE [*leaning on the balcony*]
  Well said, sir! – But your speech is strangely slow.
  What hesitation stops its easy flow?
CYRANO
  Stop, this is getting too difficult. Here!
  [*He pulls* CHRISTIAN *in under the balcony and steps out
  in his place.*]
ROXANE
  Your words are halting – why?
CYRANO [*quietly, imitating* CHRISTIAN]
                                          The night is dark.
  To reach your ears they have to feel their way.
ROXANE
  Mine can reach yours more easily, it seems.
CYRANO
  They find their way at once? That's not surprising,   210
  Since they go straight to my heart. My heart is big,
  Your ears are tiny, and your words are falling
  While mine must rise: of course it takes them longer.
ROXANE
  But now it seems they're travelling much faster.
CYRANO
  They must be learning to climb!
ROXANE
                                          And I'm so high up!
CYRANO
  A hard word dropped from there into my heart
  Would break it.
ROXANE
                      Wait, I'll come down.
CYRANO
                                          No! Don't!
ROXANE
  Stand on the bench, then.

CYRANO

No!

ROXANE

What do you mean, no?

CYRANO [*ever more moved*]

Let's just enjoy this unexpected chance
To talk together quietly, unseen.

ROXANE

220   Unseen?

CYRANO

It's charming! You hardly know who's there.
All you can see's a long, black, trailing cloak,
And I the whiteness of a summer dress.
I'm nothing but a shadow, you a gleam!
You don't know what these minutes mean to me.
Some say I have the gift of words . . .

ROXANE

You have!

CYRANO

But till this night my words have never sprung
From my true heart . . .

ROXANE

But why?

CYRANO

Because

I've always had to speak them through . . .

ROXANE

Through what?

CYRANO

230   The trembling dizziness that overtakes
The bravest man when he is in your sight.
And yet it seems to me that here, tonight,
Will be the first time I can speak to you.

ROXANE

It's true, your voice sounds different.

CYRANO

Quite different, for, under the cloak of night,
I can be my true self, and dare . . .

[*Breaking off, distractedly*]

                                              Where was I?
I don't know what . . . all this . . . forgive me, please . . .
It's so delightful for me . . . and so new!

ROXANE
  New?

CYRANO
              New . . . yes . . . saying what I feel . . .
I'm always so afraid of being laughed at . . .   240

ROXANE
  Laughed at? Why?

CYRANO
                        Oh, you know . . . enthusiasm . . .
I always hide my feelings under wit.
Longing to pluck a star down from the firmament,
Instead I stoop and pick a flowery compliment.

ROXANE
  Compliments can be fun.

CYRANO
                            But not tonight.

ROXANE
  I've never heard you talk like this before.

CYRANO
  Oh, let's leave Cupid's darts and flames alone
For once, and talk of something . . . nearer home!
Instead of sipping from a tiny cup
Of gold the Lignon's waters,[2] drop by drop,   250
Let's see what happens if we let our souls
Drink deeply of the river as it rolls!

ROXANE
  But what becomes of wit?

CYRANO
                          Oh, let it be.
How can you look for wit on such a night?
The breeze, the scents, the air – how could one turn them
Into a compliment *à la* Voiture?[3]
Let the stars work their magic, melt away
Our artificial manners, lest the alchemy

Of wit dissolve the truth of feeling.
260   These empty games will empty out our souls,
And fine-spun subtleties will one day break.

ROXANE
Wit . . .

CYRANO
            . . . Has no place in love. It's criminal
Once one's in love to draw out one's resistance.
The day must come – I pity from the heart
Those whom it never comes for – when both lovers
Will recognize the noble love between them
And see how every clever word demeans it.

ROXANE
So, if that moment now has come for us,
What words will you use to tell it?

CYRANO
                                    All of them.
270   Each word that comes to me. I'll throw them all
In sheaves at your feet, no time to make a bouquet:
I love you, I'm stifling, I love you, I'm crazy, it's more
Than I can bear. Your name's like a bell in my heart,
Dearest, a little bell, and as I keep trembling,
The bell keeps ringing and ringing and saying your name.
The tiniest things about you live in my memory.
I've loved them all, always. Last year, I remember,
On the twelfth of May, you changed the style of your hair!
You know when you look too long at the sun, the disc
280   Of fire that floats on everything afterwards? Well,
Your hair was my sunlight, and after I looked away
There were patches of blonde light all over the world.

ROXANE [touched by what she has heard]
Yes, that's love.

CYRANO
                    That feeling that overwhelms me,
Fearsome, possessive, is love all right: it has all
The madness and sadness of love, and still, it isn't
A selfish thing: God knows, I'd gladly give up

All of my hopes of happiness for yours,
Whether the news of it would ever reach you.
All I would want would be the sound of your laughter,
Heard in the distance, and knowing I'd freed you to laugh.   290
All that I need is the look in your eyes, and bravery
Springs up inside me. Does that make sense, do you
Know what I'm saying? This is my soul, in the darkness,
Reaching towards you. God, how can I bear it?
Such silence, such beauty, the dusk and the cool of the
    evening,
Me talking, you listening. Never, even in dreams
Did I hope for so much. I can die now. –

                            Wait, though –
    she's trembling!
You're trembling – for me! Under the shadowy branches
Like a leaf among leaves! I feel it, don't try to hide it,
Your marvellous trembling is shaking the jessamine
    boughs.   300
    [*He passionately kisses an overhanging branch.*]
ROXANE
It's true, I'm trembling, I'm crying, I love you, I'm yours.
My darling, I'm drunk on your words!
CYRANO
                         So now let me die.
This rapture's my doing, mine – what more could I ask for
But this? Just one thing . . .
CHRISTIAN [*from under the balcony*]
                    A kiss!
ROXANE [*shocked at first*]
                What!
CYRANO
               Oh!
ROXANE
What did you ask for?
CYRANO
            I'm sorry, forgive me . . . [*To* CHRIS-
    TIAN] How could you?

CHRISTIAN
    She's weakening, Cyrano, this was the moment!
ROXANE
                                                    You wanted . . .
CYRANO
    Forgive me, I shouldn't have . . .
ROXANE [*rather sadly*]
                                        Well, if you're sure . . .
CYRANO
                                                        I'm sure.
CHRISTIAN [*tugging* CYRANO *by his cloak*]
    Why not?
CYRANO
                Shut up, Christian.
ROXANE [*leaning out of the window*]
                            What did you say?
CYRANO
    I was scolding myself for going too far. Shut up,
    Christian, I said . . .
    [*The theorbos are heard.*]
310   Wait! I hear someone coming.
    [ROXANE *hastily closes the window.* CYRANO *listens to the
    theorbos: one is playing a cheerful and the other a plaintive
    air.*]
    One cheerful tune and one sad – what can they mean?
    Is it a man or a woman? I see, it's a monk!
    [*Enter a capuchin monk, carrying a lantern. He goes from
    house to house examining the doors.*]

Scene VIII

CYRANO, CHRISTIAN, MONK

CYRANO
You with the lantern, sir Diogenes![1]
What are you seeking?

MONK
                              Sir, the house of a lady ...

CHRISTIAN
Get rid of him!

MONK
                    ... named Madeleine Robin.

CYRANO [pointing away from the house]
It's that way, straight ahead.

MONK
                              God bless you, sir.

CYRANO
Thank you. God speed, and pray for my intentions.

Scene IX

CYRANO, CHRISTIAN

CHRISTIAN
I must have that kiss.

CYRANO
                    Not now.

CHRISTIAN
                              It has to happen.

CYRANO
Yes, I suppose it must: the time has come.
Her rosy lips must meet your blond moustache,   320
You're both so beautiful. At least my words ...

Scene X

CYRANO, CHRISTIAN, ROXANE

ROXANE [*reappearing on the balcony*]
What were we speaking of . . . ?
CYRANO
                                    A kiss, I think.
Delightful word. You needn't fear to speak it.
If the word burns your lips, what will the thing do?
Come, be brave: you'd almost finished flirting:
Moved from a smile to a sigh, from a sigh to a tear . . .
Let yourself go a little further still:
From a tear to a kiss is just a tremor away.
ROXANE
Fie!
CYRANO
        A kiss! What is a kiss? A confession
330   Made from a little closer at hand, a promise
Delivered as soon as it's made,
A secret whispered close, with a mouth to hear it:
Eternity held in a moment that stings like a bee.
Passed like communion, a host with the scent of flowers,
A way to breathe the breath of the heart of another
And with one's lips to sip the beloved one's soul.
ROXANE
For shame!
CYRANO
                A kiss is such a noble thing
The Queen of France herself did not disdain
To let the happy English noble[1] steal one.
340   Like Buckingham I suffered without speaking,
Like him let me adore you as my queen;
Faithful and sad like him . . .
ROXANE
                                    And handsome too . . .
CYRANO [*sadly*]

Handsome too. I forgot.
ROXANE

                              Come then, and gather
My own heart's breath . . .
CYRANO [*pushing* CHRISTIAN]

                              Go on!
ROXANE

                              This sweet communion . . .
CYRANO
Go on! What are you waiting for?
CHRISTIAN

                              It feels wrong.
ROXANE
Eternity . . .
CYRANO

              Go, God damn you!
      [CHRISTIAN *leaps on to the bench, scrambles up the wall
      and vaults the balustrade.*]
CHRISTIAN

                              Oh, Roxane!
      [*He takes her in his arms and kisses her.*]
CYRANO
That hurt . . . A beggar at love's banquet, still
That kiss had something in it meant for me,
Since on his lips his mistress kissed my words.
      [*The theorbos are heard again.*]
First sad, then gay: the monk again.
      [CYRANO *goes to the wings and comes back running, pre-
      tending to have come from a distance. He calls out:*]

                              I say!   350
ROXANE
Who is it?
CYRANO

              Cyrano. Is Christian there?
CHRISTIAN
Cyrano! What a surprise!
ROXANE

                    Good evening, cousin.

Wait, I'll come down.
[*She goes into the house.* MONK *reappears.*]
CHRISTIAN
                    Damn, it's the monk again.
[*Follows her.*]

Scene XI

CYRANO, CHRISTIAN, ROXANE, MONK, RAGUENEAU

MONK
I'm sorry, but they said she *does* live here:
Madeleine Robin.
CYRANO
                    But you said Ro*lin.*
MONK
No, Robin: B-I-N.
[ROXANE *appears at the door, followed by* RAGUENEAU,
carrying a lantern, and by CHRISTIAN.]
ROXANE
                    What is it?
MONK
A letter, madam.
CHRISTIAN
                    What?
MONK
                              You've nothing to fear.
It can mean only good. The worthy gentleman . . .
ROXANE [*to* CHRISTIAN]
It's from De Guiche.
CHRISTIAN
                    How dare he?
ROXANE
                              Never mind him.
It's you I love. Just let him try . . .

[*Opens letter by the light of* RAGUENEAU'*s lantern and reads.*]

Dear madam,   360

The drums are beating, and my regiment
Makes ready to depart. They think me gone,
But, flouting your sweet orders, I remain
Here in this convent, hoping for forgiveness.
Tonight I come to you. I send this letter
By a monk's hand, the simplest creature living:
He'll suspect nothing. Keep the house tonight,
Let no one enter but your humble servant.
Yours to command till death, et cetera.

[*To* MONK]

Good father, would you like to hear my letter?   370

[*All draw round to listen to her read.*]

ROXANE

Madam,

We must obey the cardinal

Despite the secret wishes of our hearts.
This worthy, subtle monk will bring my message,
Which is that you and Christian must be married
In secrecy, tonight, within your house.
This holy man will carry out the rites.
Christian is not the one you love, I know:
You must resign yourself, and heaven will bless you.
Such is the wish of your obedient servant,
Yours to command till death, et cetera.   380

MONK

The will of heaven! Worthy gentleman!

ROXANE [*aside to* CHRISTIAN]

Don't I read letters well?

[*aloud*]   Ah, 'tis too cruel!

MONK [*shining the lantern on* CHRISTIAN]

Is this the bridegroom?

CHRISTIAN

Yes.

MONK [*uncertainly, looking at him*]

But . . .

ROXANE
                              There's a postscript!
Let him have a donation for the convent:
A hundred silver pieces.
MONK
                              Worthy gentleman!
Are you resigned?
ROXANE
                    I am.
[RAGUENEAU *opens the door and* CHRISTIAN *signs to*
MONK *to go into the house.*]
ROXANE [*aside*]
                         Cyrano, quickly.
You have to stop De Guiche. Just keep him talking.
He mustn't come inside until it's over.
CYRANO
I'll deal with him.
[*To* MONK]
                    Father, how long does it take
To marry a couple?
MONK
                         A quarter of an hour.
CYRANO
If you'll excuse me, friends, I'll stay out here.
[*All others enter house.*]

Scene XII

     CYRANO

CYRANO
How can I stop De Guiche? . . . I've an idea!
[*He jumps up on the bench and climbs the wall towards
the balcony. Theorbos are heard again – a major tune this
time.*]

A man!

[*A sinister tremolo on the theorbos.*]

    It's him.

[CYRANO *has reached the balcony. He lowers his hat over his eyes, lays down his sword and wraps himself in his cloak. Then he takes hold of a strong branch of the tree and prepares to launch himself into space.*]

    Let's give him a surprise.

Scene XIII

CYRANO, DE GUICHE

Enter DE GUICHE, *masked, feeling his way.*

DE GUICHE

Where's that damned monk!

CYRANO

                    My voice! What if he knows me!

Must turn my accent on again.[1]

[*Mimes turning a key in his chest*]

                       Krk, krk.

DE GUICHE

That's the house. Damn this mask!

[*As he goes to enter the house,* CYRANO *swings down on the branch, landing between him and the door. He pretends to land very heavily, and lies on the ground as if knocked out.*]

DE GUICHE [*starting*]

                      Who's that?

Where did you land from?

CYRANO [*sitting up, Scottish accent*]

                From the moon.

DE GUICHE

                      The *moon*?

CYRANO
    What's the time?
DE GUICHE
                        The time? He's lost his senses.
CYRANO
    The time, the day, the month, the year? Where are we?
400 My head's all spinnin'. It's a long way, ye ken,
    From here to the moon.
DE GUICHE
                        Of course it is.
    [*shrinking away from him*]
                                    He's mad.
CYRANO
    A hundred year ago, or just a minute,
    I was up there, ye ken, in yon big ball.
DE GUICHE
    Of course you were. And now, if you'll excuse me . . .
CYRANO [*still blocking his way*]
    Don't be afraid to tell me where we are:
    I didn't have a choice of where I landed.
    Is this another moon or is it Earth
    My bum has landed on?
DE GUICHE
    My dear good man, I tell you . . .
CYRANO [*pretending to be frightened*]
                                Help ma boab!
410 They've all got black faces here! Is this Africa?
DE GUICHE
    It's a mask!
CYRANO [*reassured*]
                Aw, is it Venice, then?
DE GUICHE
                                Please!
    I have to meet a lady.
CYRANO
                Got it! It's Paris.
DE GUICHE [*smiling in spite of himself*]
    You're not so crazy, then.

CYRANO

                              I made ye laugh.

DE GUICHE

  Now you can let me pass.

CYRANO

                              Ye must excuse me,
  I'm no exactly dressed for Paris, since
  I just blew in on the planetary wind.
  The stardust's still about me – what a journey!
  Look, on my jerkin sleeve, a comet's hair.

DE GUICHE

  Let me pass . . .

CYRANO

                    Look at the Great Bear's tooth
  Stuck in my calf. And when I passed the Trident   420
  I took a swerve to miss one of its prongs
  And landed in the Scales: I daresay they
  Can still read my weight up there.

    [DE GUICHE *again tries to pass but* CYRANO *blocks his
    way, buttonholing him.*]

CYRANO

                              See my nose?
  Squeeze it! Ye know what'll come out? Milk!

DE GUICHE

  Milk?

CYRANO

        From the Milky Way.

DE GUICHE

                              Hell and damnation!

CYRANO

  No, I'm sent from heaven! Would ye believe
      [*Confidentially*]
  Sirius wears a nightcap? The Little Bear[2]
  Is still cutting its teeth. I broke a string
  As I went through the Lyre . . . But there,
      [*Grandly*]
  I'll write it all down when I write my book.   430
  And when it's printed out, all the wee stars

Stuck to my cloak will do for asterisks.
Look, let me show you . . .
DE GUICHE
                                    Will you let me pass?
CYRANO [*conspiratorially*]
I know what you would like to know . . .
DE GUICHE
                                    Oh, please!
CYRANO
The moon! What is it made of? And the wee man,
Does he really live there?
DE GUICHE
                        No, I *only want* . . .
CYRANO
To know how I got up there! Well, I'll tell you.
The method's all my own.
DE GUICHE
                            He *is* mad.
CYRANO
                                    Not the eagle
Regiomontanus tried to harness, nor the pigeon
440   Archytas used – I knew that wouldn't work.
DE GUICHE [*aside*]
A madman, but a learned madman . . .
CYRANO
                            No,
I never imitated all those others.
        [DE GUICHE *has got past* CYRANO *and is moving towards*
        ROXANE's *door*. CYRANO *follows him, ready to stop him.*]
Instead I found six methods of my own[3]
To penetrate the heavens' secrets . . .
DE GUICHE [*despairing*]
                                    Six?
CYRANO [*brightly*]
Of course, I could have taken all my clothes off,
And covered all my skin in wee glass bottles
Filled up with dewdrops. When I stood in the sun
I'd have been lifted up with the morning vapour.

DE GUICHE [*interested in spite of himself*]
    Well, that's one way.
CYRANO
                            I could have captured wind
    Inside a wooden chest by heating mirrors,   450
    And used its force to blow me to the skies.
DE GUICHE
    Two.
        [*As* DE GUICHE *becomes more fascinated,* CYRANO *draws
        him after him around the stage.*]
CYRANO
            I could have built a metal grasshopper,
    On springs, and used a charge of saltpetre[4]
    To fire me into space.
DE GUICHE
                            Three.
CYRANO
                                Since smoke rises,
    I could have filled a globe and ridden on it.
DE GUICHE
    Four.
CYRANO
        Animals' marrow, as we know,
    Is drawn towards the waning moon, and so
    I could have rubbed it over all my skin.
DE GUICHE
    What! Er ... five ...
        [*By this time* CYRANO *has lured* DE GUICHE *to a bench at
        the other side of the square.*]
CYRANO
                        Another good idea:
    Stand on a metal plate, and throw a magnet   460
    Into the air. The plate will rise to meet it;
    Throw it again, again, and so by stages
    Up to the moon.
DE GUICHE
                    That *is* an idea. Tell me,
    Which of the six did you choose?

CYRANO

None of them.

See if ye can guess the seventh.

DE GUICHE

You know, he's got something!

CYRANO

Here, let me give ye a clue:

[*Waving his arms wildly and imitating the sound of waves*]

Woo! woo!

DE GUICHE

What?

CYRANO

I'll give ye three guesses.

DE GUICHE

I give up.

CYRANO

The tide, man! The moon draws up the tide at night
470   So I went for a swim and then lay out on the sand.
My hair was full of water so that went up
The first, the rest of me followed, floating away
Just like an angel, until . . .

DE GUICHE [*sitting on the bench, completely under* CYRANO'*s spell*]

Until . . .

CYRANO [*in his normal voice*]

Time's up.

Your quarter hour is over, and they're married.

DE GUICHE [*leaping to his feet*]

What! Am I mad? That voice!

[*The door opens, footmen come out bearing lighted candlesticks.* CYRANO *takes off his hat.*]

DE GUICHE

And that nose! Cyrano!

CYRANO [*bowing*]

The wedding is complete.

DE GUICHE

Whose wedding?

[*The wedding party comes out of the house:* ROXANE *and*

CHRISTIAN *holding hands, the* MONK *walking behind them smiling approvingly,* RAGUENEAU *carrying another candlestick and* DUENNA *bringing up the rear in her dressing-gown.*]

DE GUICHE

Curses!

Scene XIV

CYRANO, DE GUICHE, ROXANE, CHRISTIAN, MONK, RAGUENEAU, DUENNA

DE GUICHE
You, Roxane!
[*Recognizing* CHRISTIAN, *amazed*]
And you!
[*Sarcastically*]
Congratulations!
A well-laid plan. My compliments to you
As well, the lunar traveller. Your tales
Would stop a freed soul on its way to heaven.   480
You really ought to publish them some day.

CYRANO
I will.

MONK
You've done God's work, most worthy sir,
Bringing this happy pair together.

DE GUICHE
Quite.
Now, madam, you may bid your spouse goodbye.

ROXANE
Goodbye?

DE GUICHE
The regiment is leaving. You, sir,
Make ready to go with it.

ROXANE
                              To the war?
  But the cadets ...
DE GUICHE
                    I have the orders here.
  Take them to your commander, baron.
ROXANE [*rushing into* CHRISTIAN'*s arms*]
                                        Christian!
DE GUICHE [*to* CYRANO, *enjoying his victory*]
  The wedding night will have to wait a while.
CYRANO [*aside*]
  That won't break *my* heart.
CHRISTIAN
490   Darling, one more kiss!
CYRANO
  Come on, it's time to go.
CHRISTIAN [*still embracing* ROXANE]
                        But you don't know ...
CYRANO
  I can imagine.
    [*Drumbeats in the distance: the regiment is mustering.*]
DE GUICHE
                      There they go.
    [CYRANO *tries to lead* CHRISTIAN *towards the drums, but*
    ROXANE *keeps hold of his hand and tries to pull him back*
    at each line.]
ROXANE
                        Oh, Cyrano,
  You will look after him!
CYRANO
                      I'll do my best.
ROXANE
  Don't let him feel the cold out there!
CYRANO
                              I'll try.
ROXANE
  He mustn't look at any other women!

CYRANO
    I'm sure he won't.
ROXANE
                    And promise me he'll write
    A letter every day.
CYRANO [*stops pulling and stands still*]
                    That I *can* promise.

ACT IV

THE GASCONY CADETS

The scene is the position occupied by CARBON DE CASTEL-JALOUX's *company at the siege of Arras.*

Upstage, an embankment across the full width of the stage. Beyond it, a vista of flat countryside covered in siege works. In the distance, the walls of Arras and the roofs of the city silhouetted against the sky. In the foreground, tents, piles of weapons, drums, etc. It is nearly dawn: yellow light to the east. Here and there sentinels, watch-fires. Wrapped in their cloaks, the cadets are sleeping on the ground. CARBON DE CASTEL-JALOUX *and* LE BRET *are watching. They are very pale and have grown very thin.* CHRISTIAN *is asleep downstage, wrapped in his cloak, his face lit by the fire. Silence.*

Scene I

CHRISTIAN, CARBON DE CASTEL-JALOUX, LE BRET, CADETS, *then* CYRANO

LE BRET
  This is appalling.
CARBON
  　　　　　Nothing left to eat.
LE BRET
  God damn it!

CARBON [*hushing him*]
          If you must curse, do it quietly.
     You'll wake them up.
        [A CADET *stirs*]
                              Shh, go to sleep, it's nothing.
     [*To* LE BRET]
     If they can't eat, at least let them sleep it out.
LE BRET
     And if they can't sleep, too bad.
        [*Noise of gunfire.*]
CARBON
                                   Damn that gunfire!
     They'll wake my babies . . . Shh, go back to sleep!
        [*Gunfire nearer.*]
A CADET [*waking*]
     Hell, is it them?
CARBON
                    No, it's just Cyrano.
A SENTRY [*offstage*]
     Who goes there?
CYRANO
                    Bergerac.
SENTRY
                              Who goes there,
     Damn you?
CYRANO [*appearing on top of the embankment*]
                    Bergerac, idiot!
        [*As he comes down the embankment,* LE BRET *hurries
        towards him.*]
LE BRET
                              Where have you been?
CYRANO
     Shh!
LE BRET
          Are you wounded?
CYRANO
                         No, of course I'm not.   10
     They miss me every morning.

LE BRET
                                You must be mad
To cross the line like that, just for a letter.
CYRANO [*looking at* CHRISTIAN]
  I promised he would send one every day.
  Look at him, he's so pale – but still so handsome!
  If the poor child knew he's starving . . .
LE BRET
                                            We're all starving.
  You go and get some sleep.
CYRANO
                          Don't nag, Le Bret.
  I've found a place to cross the Spanish lines:
  They're always drunk.
LE BRET
                          You might have brought some food.
CYRANO
  Too much to carry. But I heard them say
20 There'll be movement tonight. Tonight we'll eat or die.
  I saw . . .
LE BRET
        What?
CYRANO
              No, I'm not sure . . .
CARBON
                                    It's too bad
  To be on the besieging side, and starving!
LE BRET
  This siege of ours is hellish complicated:
  We're besieging Arras, but now the Spaniards
  Are laying siege to us.
CYRANO
                  If only someone
  Would start besieging them!
LE BRET
                      It's not a joke!
  We need you here, why must you risk your life
  Each day, just for a letter – where are you going?

CYRANO
It's time to go and write another one.
[*He lifts the flap and disappears into a tent.*]

Scene II

CHARACTERS AS BEFORE, *minus* CYRANO

*Dawn is breaking (pink lights), gilding the roofs and spires
of Arras in the distance. Offstage R, far away, a cannon
shot followed by drumbeats. More drumbeats nearer at
hand. The gun batteries seem to be answering each other
and coming nearer to the stage. They pass behind the
embankment and eventually disappear, stage L. Bugle
calls, officers' voices in the distance.*

CARBON [*sighing*]
Reveille, more's the pity.
[*Cadets begin to stir and stretch under their cloaks.*]
        When they wake   30
I know the first thing they'll say . . .

A CADET [*sitting up*]
           God, I'm hungry!

ANOTHER CADET
I'm starving!

ANOTHER
     So am I, man!

CARBON
       Rise and shine!

ANOTHER CADET
Not today, thanks!

ANOTHER [*looking at his reflection in a breastplate*]
      Look, my tongue's all yellow!

ANOTHER
Some beef! Some beef! My barony for beef,
Or even horse! If I don't eat today,
My noble form will simply fade away!

ANOTHER
    Some bread at least!
CARBON [*quietly, speaking into the tent*]
                        Cyrano!
SEVERAL CADETS
                                    We're starving!
CARBON
    Come out! I need you here, you can distract them,
    Make them laugh . . .
SECOND CADET [*to another, who seems to be nibbling*]
                        Hey, what are you eating?
FIRST CADET
40 Some cannon oakum fried in axle grease.
    There's not much game in these parts.
        [*Enter another two cadets, separately.*]
CADET I
                                    But I've been hunting!
CADET 2
    And I've been fishing in the Scarpe.
        [*All the others run towards them.*]
CADETS
                            Let's see! –
    What have you caught? – Show us! – A pike? – A pheasant?
CADET 2
    A stickleback!
CADET I
            A sparrow!
CADETS
                        It's too bad! –
    We can't go on like this! – Cyrano, help!

Scene III

CHARACTERS AS BEFORE, *plus* CYRANO

CYRANO *emerges from his tent in leisurely fashion, with a pen behind his ear and a book in his hand.*

CYRANO
What's the matter?
[*To a* CADET *who is moving away*]
                    Where do you think you're going?
CADET
My foot had gone to sleep. I had to move it.
CYRANO
Really.
CADET
            My gut was aching.
CYRANO
                    So is mine.
It makes me stand the taller.
ANOTHER CADET
                    My teeth are on edge.
CYRANO
Get them into the Spaniards.
ANOTHER CADET
                    My belly's like a drum.   50
CYRANO
Good! We can beat the charge on it.
ANOTHER CADET
                                    I dream
Of food, of something to devour!
CYRANO [*throwing him his book*]
                    Try this –
The Iliad!
ANOTHER CADET
            The Cardinal's not starving!
Richelieu's eating his four meals a day,
I bet!

CYRANO
                 Would you like him to send you some?
CADET
    Why not? Partridge and wine.
CYRANO
                              A fine Bordeaux . . .
CADET
    By personal messenger.
CYRANO
                         Yes, the Graves eminence.[1]
ANOTHER CADET
    You've an answer for everything, Cyrano –
    Always scoring your point.[2]
CYRANO
                            My point, yes.
60 And when it's time to go, I want to fall
    For a noble cause, run through by a worthy foe,
    Out on the field of glory and not in a sickbed:
    To die with a point on my lips and a point in my heart.
ALL THE CADETS
    We're hungry!
CYRANO
                     Oh, you think of nothing but food!
    Here, you piper, pick up your fife and play us
    One of the shepherd's airs from the old country,
    Sweet and familiar, rising like cottage smoke
    Through the evening air.
    [*The old man begins to assemble his fife.*]
                              Let her forget the war,
    Your ebony flute, under your dancing fingers,
70 And call to mind the other fingers that carved her
    Out of a rustic reed, in days gone by.
    [*The piper starts to play a Gascon air.*]
    Listen, my Gascon friends. No warlike fife,
    It's a woodland flute he's playing, slow and sweet
    Like the tunes our goatherds play at evening. Listen.
    It's the sound of the valleys, the heaths and forests of home.

[*All are listening pensively, eyes are far away, and the odd tear is wiped away on a sleeve or the edge of a cloak.*]

CARBON [*under his breath, to* CYRANO]
Stop, you're making them cry!

CYRANO
                              They're homesick, bless them:
Still, it's better than crying from hunger. Their guts
Aren't griping now, the song is tugging their heartstrings.

CARBON
You'll weaken them.

CYRANO
                              No, they're all of fighting stock.
[*He beckons the drummer over.*]
Just watch.
[*Drum-roll.*]

CADETS [*jumping to their feet, grabbing their weapons*]
                    Hey! – What? – What is it? – Come on!   80

CYRANO
See, one drum-roll's enough. Home is forgotten,
Love, family, dreams – the flute did it all
And the drum undoes it.

A CADET [*looking beyond the embankment*]
                              Here comes Monsieur de Guiche!
[*Cadets groan quietly.*]

CYRANO [*smiling*]
How they admire him!

A CADET
                    What does he want here?

ANOTHER CADET
Look at him – starched lace collar over his armour!

ANOTHER
Where does he think he is, at the King's levee?

FIRST CADET
Perhaps he's got a pimple on his neck!

SECOND CADET
Man, what a courtier!

THIRD CADET
                    He's his uncle's nephew

And no mistake.

CARBON

He is a Gascon, though.

FIRST CADET

90   Don't you believe it. Gascons are all crazy.
A reasonable Gascon is a menace.

LE BRET

Isn't he pale!

SECOND CADET

He's hungry too, I guess,
Under his breastplate with its golden rivets
Glittering in the sun.

CYRANO

Then let's be like him!
Don't let them see us suffer. Pipes, dice, cards –
Get a game going . . .

[*The cadets quickly produce dice and cards, set them out
on drums, stools, etc., and light their pipes.*]

. . . while I read Descartes.[3]

[*The cadets are quickly engrossed in their games.* CYRANO
*produces a little book from his pocket and walks up and
down reading it. Tableau.*]

Scene IV

SAME CHARACTERS, *plus* DE GUICHE

DE GUICHE [*to* CARBON]
Good day, sir.

[*They study each other's appearance.*]

DE GUICHE [*aside*]

He looks dreadful.

CARBON [*ditto*]

What a colour!

DE GUICHE

So these are my admirers. Yes, gentlemen,

You Gascon nobles, Perigordin barons,
Mountain squireens, I hear you are offended   100
By your colonel's manners. You call me courtier,
Palace intriguer; you can hardly bear
To see me wearing lace over my breastplate,
As if a Gascon had to be a beggar!
Now, shall I have your captain punish you?
No, I don't think so.

CARBON
                        Sir, I would point out,
Deciding punishments is my concern.
I bought my company and I'll command it.

DE GUICHE
Will you indeed?
    [*To cadets*]
                    Your jokes at my expense
Are futile. The whole army knows my courage,   110
They saw me charge the Comte de Bucquoi yesterday,
My men against his, three times . . .

CYRANO [*his nose still in his book*]
                            And your white sash?

DE GUICHE
You heard about that? At the head of my troops
I was preparing to charge, when a fleeing rabble
Pushed me out of the line. I might have been shot
There and then, if not for my presence of mind.
Untying my colonel's sash, I threw it aside,
Gathered my troops together, charged, and broke through.
What do you say to that?
    [*The cadets seem not to be listening; but at this point the
    cards and dice-boxes are halted in mid air, the smokers
    hold the smoke in their cheeks. A pause.*]

CYRANO
                        I hardly think
King Henry would have doffed his white panache[1]   120
In any danger.
    [*Silent jubilation among the cadets. Cards, dice-boxes
    move again, smoke is exhaled.*]

DE GUICHE

        It worked, though.

   [*Suspense again.*]

CYRANO

                No doubt.

But it's a source of pride to be a target.

   [*Delight again, movement resumed.*]

If I had been at hand when the sash fell –

So different are our temperaments, my lord –

I would have picked it up and wrapped it round me.

DE GUICHE

Typical Gascon boasting!

CYRANO

                So you say.

Lend it to me, I'll put it on today

And charge the enemy with it about me.

DE GUICHE

More Gascon bluff! You know it's lost, I dropped it

In the thick of the fight, where no one could retrieve it.

CYRANO [*taking the sash from his pocket and holding it out*
    to DE GUICHE]

Is this it?

   [*Silence. The cadets try to suppress their laughter.* DE
   GUICHE *turns and stares at them; they straighten their
   faces and ostentatiously resume their games. One casually
   whistles the mountain air the piper has just played.*]

DE GUICHE

        Thank you. Now I can use it

To make a signal.

   [*He climbs up the embankment and waves the white sash.*]

ALL

              What!

SENTRY [*on the embankment*]

           A spy, running off!

DE GUICHE [*coming down*]

The man's a double agent. I provide him

With information he takes back to base.

So we control the enemy's decisions.

CYRANO
A villain!
DE GUICHE [*nonchalantly tying his sash on again*]
            Yes, but useful. We were saying . . .
Oh, yes. I had some news for you. Last night
Supplies arrived from Paris, and the Marshal
Has gone to meet the waggons near Doullens.
Half of the troops are with him, so the camp   140
Is almost undefended. What a moment
To launch an attack!
CARBON
                    Yes, if the Spaniards knew it,
But they don't.
DE GUICHE
                    They do. They'll come in force today.
My double agent came to give me warning
And let me choose where the attack would be.
He'll tell the Spaniards that's the weakest point,
And that's where they'll come. I said, 'Look down the line,
And where you see me signal, that's the spot.'
CARBON
Cadets, prepare to fight.
    [*They jump to their feet, begin buckling on their sword-
    belts.*]
DE GUICHE
                    You have an hour.
A CADET
Oh, well, in that case . . .
    [*All sit down and resume their games.*]
DE GUICHE
                            Captain, we must gain time   150
And hold them off until the Marshal comes.
CARBON
How will we do that?
DE GUICHE
                    Stand your ground, and die.
CYRANO
So this is your revenge?

DE GUICHE
                              I won't pretend
That, if I liked you more, I would have chosen
You for this sacrifice, but since the world
Knows your mad bravery, I can say I'm serving
The royal interest as I serve my own.
CYRANO [saluting]
   You do us too much honour, sir.
DE GUICHE [returning the salute]
                                     I know
You love to fight against unlikely odds.
160   A hundred to one, eh? You'll enjoy today.
      [He retreats upstage with CARBON. They talk sotto voce.
      Meanwhile CYRANO speaks to the cadets.]
CYRANO
   Gentlemen, to the arms of Gascony –
   Six chevrons, or and azure – here today
   We'll add a chevron gules,[2] painted in blood.
      [He goes to CHRISTIAN and puts a hand on his shoulder.]
CYRANO
   Christian?
CHRISTIAN [shaking his head]
                  Roxane!
CYRANO
                        Poor child!
CHRISTIAN
                              If only I
Could put my dearest feelings in a letter!
CYRANO
   I thought they might attack today, and so
   I wrote the letter for you.
      [Extracts the letter from his doublet.]
CHRISTIAN
                        Let me see!
CYRANO
   Are you sure?
CHRISTIAN
                  Of course!

[*Takes it and opens it.*]
                              But Cyrano, what's that?

CYRANO
  What's what?

CHRISTIAN
                    That little round thing – it's a tear-stain!

CYRANO [*taking back the letter*]
  Perhaps it is. You know what poets are –   170
  We make ourselves believe in what we write.
  It *was* a sad letter, and it made me cry.

CHRISTIAN
  Cry? You?

CYRANO
                    You know, it's not the thought of dying,
  But never seeing her again, that's dreadful.
  And I will – I mean, we will – that is, you will . . .

CHRISTIAN [*increasingly uneasy*]
  Give me the letter. [*Grabs it back.*]
    [*Noises off.*]

SENTRY [*on the embankment*]
                              Who goes there?
    [*Shouts, voices, jingling of harness.*]

CARBON
                                         What is it?

SENTRY
  A carriage!
    [*All rush to the top of the embankment, jostling for a
    view.*]

VOICES
                    What! In the camp? – It's coming in –
  From the Spanish side – Shoot! – No! – Who is it? –
  What did the coachman say? – On the King's service!

DE GUICHE
  The King! Make way, make way at once!   180
    [*All rush down from the embankment and begin to form
    a guard of honour.*]

CARBON
  Cadets, salute!

[*The carriage appears, covered in mud and dust. All doff their hats.*]

CARBON

Lower the steps!

[*Two men rush to open the carriage door.* ROXANE *appears at the head of the steps.*]

ROXANE

Hello, boys!

[*At the sound of a woman's voice, all the men, still bowing low, raise their heads in astonishment.*]

Scene V

SAME CHARACTERS, *plus* ROXANE, RAGUENEAU

DE GUICHE

On the King's service! You?

ROXANE

The king of hearts,

Cupid himself.

CYRANO

God help us!

CHRISTIAN [*rushing towards her*].

Why did you come?

ROXANE

I'd had enough of writing.

CYRANO [*stock still, his eyes turned away*].

I can't look at her.

DE GUICHE

You can't stay: this is madness.

ROXANE

Yes I can.

Somebody give me a drum.

[*A* CADET *brings forward a drum; she sits on it.*]

Thanks. [*Proudly*] Do you know,

They shot at my coach! Yes, a Spanish patrol.

It looks like Cinderella's carriage, doesn't it,
Made from a pumpkin, with white mice for footmen.
   [*Blowing a kiss to* CHRISTIAN]
Christian, my darling!
   [*Looking more closely at the others*]
                        Don't you all look glum!   190
I tell you, it's a long, long way to Arras!
   [*Noticing* CYRANO]
Cyrano, how delightful!

CYRANO
                 How did you get here?

ROXANE
How did I find the army? It was easy.
I kept on travelling. When I saw the ruins
I knew the war couldn't be far away.
I wouldn't have believed it till I saw it.
Horrors! If that's the service of your King,
 You're better off with mine.

CYRANO
                   I can't believe it.
How did you cross the Spanish lines?

ROXANE
                         Quite simply.
I just kept trotting through. If someone stopped me   200
I'd show my face at the window, smiling sweetly,
And since no Spaniard can resist a lady
They'd stop to talk.

CARBON
             That smile's the best of passports.
But then they must have asked where you were going.

ROXANE
Of course, and I'd reply, 'To see my lover',
And then even the fiercest-looking Spaniard
Would close the carriage door, and with a gesture
Of regal dignity call off the guns
Already trained on me, and bow me through.
How elegant they are, what perfect manners!   210
Those massive ruffs, those hats with flying plumes –

I was quite bowled over.

CHRISTIAN

Roxane!

ROXANE

Sorry, darling!
I shouldn't have said lover, but you know
It wouldn't have had quite the same effect
If I'd said husband.

DE GUICHE

Quite, but now you must go.

ROXANE

Go?

CYRANO

Yes, at once!

LE BRET

Immediately!

CHRISTIAN

Yes!

ROXANE

But why?

CHRISTIAN [hesitantly]

Well, you see . . .

CYRANO [ditto]

In an hour or so . . .

DE GUICHE [ditto]

There may be things . . .

CARBON [ditto]

. . . You wouldn't like to see.

ROXANE

I understand. You're going to fight. I'll stay.
If Christian dies, I want to die beside him.

DE GUICHE

But the position's hopeless!

CYRANO

And that's why
He's given it to us.

ROXANE [to DE GUICHE]

I see. Your plan

Was to make me a widow.
DE GUICHE
                              No, I swear . . .
ROXANE
Now I *am* mad. I won't leave. Anyway
This looks like fun.
CYRANO
                    Who would have thought it? Now
The young *précieuse* turns out to be a heroine.
ROXANE
Remember I'm your cousin, Cyrano.
CADETS
We'll all defend you.
ROXANE [*enthusiastically*]
                              Why, of course you will.
A CADET [*ditto*]
Your perfume's scenting all the camp!
ROXANE
                                        And look,
  Isn't this hat just perfect for a battle?   230
    [*Looking towards* DE GUICHE]
It's time Monsieur de Guiche was moving on,
Perhaps – the fighting could start any minute.
DE GUICHE
How dare you! I will go and check the cannon
And come directly back – but you, I beg you,
Let me persuade you to go home.
ROXANE
                              Never!
                                   [*Exit* DE GUICHE.]

Scene VI

SAME CHARACTERS, *minus* DE GUICHE

CHRISTIAN [*imploringly*]

                                        Roxane!

ROXANE
  No.

FIRST CADET
    She's staying.

SECOND CADET
                    Gentlemen, we've a guest.

CADETS
    Quick, a comb! – Soap! – There's a hole in my doublet! –
    Who's got a needle? – Let me borrow your mirror! –
    My cuffs! – Your curling-iron! – A razor here!

ROXANE [*to* CYRANO]
240 Cyrano, I'm not going and that's that.
        [CARBON *too has been smartening himself up. He
        approaches* ROXANE.]

CARBON [*ceremoniously*].
    Madam, will you permit me to present
    Some of the gentlemen who'll have the honour,
    Later today, to die before your eyes?
        [ROXANE *bows and stands waiting for the introductions,
        leaning on* CHRISTIAN'*s arm.*]

CARBON
    Baron de Pesceyrous de Colignac.[1]
        [CADET *bows.*]
    Baron de Casterac de Cahuzac –
    Vidame de Malgouyre Lesbas d'Escarabiot –
    Chevalier d'Antignac-Juzet – Baron
    De Blagnac-Salechan de Crabioules –

ROXANE
    So many names!

BARON DE BLAGNAC
                    And all so glorious!

CARBON

Dear lady, would you drop your handkerchief?   250

ROXANE

My handkerchief? With pleasure, sir, but why?

[*She drops it and all the cadets scramble to pick it up.*]

CARBON

To make a standard for my company.

ROXANE [*smiling*]

It's rather small for that!

CARBON

But such fine lace!

[*He fastens the handkerchief to the point of his captain's lance.*]

ONE CADET [*to another*]

I could die happy looking on that face,

If only I had something in my belly!

CARBON [*overhearing*]

For shame! To think of eating when a lady . . .

ROXANE

I'm hungry too, captain: the air is sharp.

So let's eat something – a pie, some cold meat, wine?

[*Consternation among the cadets.*]

CADETS

Where will we find all that?

ROXANE

Why, in my carriage.

ALL

What!

ROXANE

Just a moment, I want to serve it properly.   260

Everything must be carved, the bones removed.

Let's call my coachman – you may recognize him.

[RAGUENEAU *appears on the box of the coach.*]

CADETS

It's Ragueneau! Three cheers for Ragueneau!

ROXANE [*looking towards the cadets*]

Poor souls!

CYRANO [*kissing her hand*]
        You're like a fairy godmother!
RAGUENEAU [*standing on the box and orating like a
    mountebank*]
    Gentlemen!
CADETS
        Hurrah! Silence for Ragueneau!
RAGUENEAU
    Snared by the brilliance of my lady's eyes
    The Spaniards let the food pass in disguise.
    [*Applause.* CYRANO *tries to attract* CHRISTIAN's *atten-
    tion.*]
    Their gallantry let through the galantine.
    [*More applause. The galantine is handed down from the
    coach and passed round.*]
CYRANO
    Christian, a word . . .
RAGUENEAU
             The power of Venus won
270   A passage for Diana's venison.
    [*He brandishes a haunch of venison. More applause, the
    venison is quickly passed from hand to hand.*]
CYRANO [*to* CHRISTIAN]
    We have to talk.
    [*The cadets lift food down from the coach.*]
ROXANE
        Put it down there, that's right.
    [*She begins to spread a cloth on the ground, helped by two
    impassive footmen who had been riding behind the coach.
    *CYRANO *has managed to draw* CHRISTIAN *aside, but
    *ROXANE *spots him and calls him to her.*]
ROXANE
    Christian, make yourself useful.
    [*He goes to her.* CYRANO *looks worried.*]
RAGUENEAU
                 Truffled peacock!
FIRST CADET [*ecstatic, cutting himself a slice of ham*]
    Truffled peacock! Well, if we have to die,

At least we'll die with something in our bellies . . .
   [*seeing* ROXANE]
Stomachs, excuse me.

RAGUENEAU [*throwing down the carriage cushions*]
                    Here are the cushions, catch!
They're stuffed with ortolans.

SECOND CADET
                         God's blood and bones!
   [*The cushions are ripped open. Laughter, excitement.*]

RAGUENEAU [*throwing down bottles*]
   Here's ruby-red . . .
   [*Throws more*]
                    And topaz-yellow wine!

ROXANE [*throwing a folded tablecloth to* CYRANO]
   Lay the cloth, quickly . . .

RAGUENEAU [*brandishing a carriage-lamp*]
                  . . . And the lamps, each one's
A tiny larder.

CYRANO [*to* CHRISTIAN, *as they spread the cloth together*]
                Christian, I must talk to you
Before you talk to her.

RAGUENEAU
                 Even the handle   280
Of my coachman's whip is an Arles sausage!

ROXANE [*always moving, pouring out wine, serving food*]
   They mean to kill us, do they? Well, to hell
With all the rest of the army. They can starve.
This is the Gascons' feast, and if De Guiche
Should dare to show his face, he's not invited! –
Go on, take your time, there's plenty more –
Now have some wine – You're crying! What's the matter?

FIRST CADET
   It's all too good.

ROXANE
            Quiet! – More bread here, please,
For Monsieur Carbon. – A knife here! – Pass your plate! –
A piece of pie-crust? What can I cut for you? –   290
A little more? – Some burgundy? – A wing?

CYRANO [*laden with plates, helping* ROXANE *to serve, to himself*]

Isn't she wonderful!

ROXANE [*to* CHRISTIAN]

                              What would *you* like?

CHRISTIAN

                                        Nothing.

ROXANE

Oh, but you must! A biscuit, in some wine?

CHRISTIAN [*trying to hold her back*]

Why did you come? Will you tell me?

ROXANE

                              In a moment

I must look after the boys.

[LE BRET *is upstage, passing a loaf on the point of a lance to the sentinel on duty.*]

LE BRET

                    Here comes De Guiche!

CYRANO

Quick, put it all away, he mustn't suspect . . .

Ragueneau, back on your box. Is everything gone?

[*In an instant everything has been whisked away into tents, under clothes, in hats.* DE GUICHE *strides on, stops, sniffs the air. Silence.*]

Scene VII

SAME CHARACTERS, *plus* DE GUICHE

DE GUICHE

Something smells good!

[*A* CADET *hums in an offhand manner.*]

                    What's this? Your face is red.

CADET

My blood is up, sir, thinking of the battle.

ANOTHER CADET
  Te tum, te tum ...
DE GUICHE
                    What did you say?
CADET [*slightly drunk*]
                                        Sorry, sir,   300
  I was singing.
DE GUICHE
              Singing! I'm glad you're so cheerful.
CADET
  Must keep our spirits up!
DE GUICHE [*calling* CARBON *over to give him orders*]
                    Captain, I ... Damn it!
  You look cheerful as well.
    [CARBON, *red in the face, is hiding a bottle behind his
    back.*]
                              Now, our last cannon ...
  I've had them bring it here – it may be useful.
A CADET
  Charming! How kind!
ANOTHER [*same manner*]
                    He really does look after us!
DE GUICHE
  Mad! They're all mad!
    [*Drily, to the company*]
                        Now, none of you are gunners,
  So watch for the recoil.
A CADET
                    Pooh! Rubbish!
DE GUICHE
                                        What!
CADET
  Our Gascon cannon don't recoil from anything.
DE GUICHE
  This man is drunk – on what?
CADET [*grandly*]
                    The scent of battle.

DE GUICHE [*despairing of him, turns to* ROXANE]
    Madam, you must decide.
ROXANE
                    I'll stay.
DE GUICHE
                        Please go.
310
ROXANE
    No.
DE GUICHE
    In that case, someone give me a musket.
CARBON
    What?
DE GUICHE
      I'm staying too.
CYRANO
               Now that *is* courage.
FIRST CADET [*to* DE GUICHE]
    Under that lace, could you be a Gascon too?
ROXANE
    You mean . . .
DE GUICHE
          How could I leave a woman in danger?
SECOND CADET [*to the* FIRST]
    The man deserves some food, what do you say?
    [*The food and drink reappear as if by a miracle.* DE
    GUICHE'*s eyes light up, but he controls himself.*]
DE GUICHE [*haughtily*]
    What, do you think I'm going to eat your leavings?
CYRANO
    I like that. Good!
DE GUICHE
          I don't need food to fight.
    [*He pronounces 'food' with a slight Scottish 'oo'.*]
FIRST CADET [*delighted, using same pronunciation*]
    Food! He *is* one of us!
DE GUICHE [*laughing*]
              Nonsense!

THE CADET
                              You are!
  [*All cadets dance with delight.* CARBON, *who had dis-
  appeared earlier, reappears from behind the embankment,
  above which a row of helmets and pikes can now be seen.*]
CARBON
  The pikemen are drawn up, they'll stand their ground.
DE GUICHE
  Will you review them, madam?
  [*He offers her his hand, which she takes, and they walk in
  stately fashion towards the embankment, followed by all
  the company except* CYRANO *and* CHRISTIAN, *who remain
  downstage.*]
CHRISTIAN
                              Cyrano!   320
A VOICE [*behind the embankment*]
  To the lady, present . . . arms!
  [*The pikes are lowered.* ROXANE *bows.*]
CHRISTIAN
                              Tell me now.
CYRANO
  Well, if Roxane mentions the letters . . .
CHRISTIAN
                              Letters!
CYRANO
  Don't let her see you're surprised.
CHRISTIAN
                              Surprised at what?
CYRANO
  I should have talked to you about it sooner.
  I didn't think till now . . . You see, you've sent her . . .
  More letters than you thought.
CHRISTIAN
                              What!
CYRANO
                              Yes.
  I said that I would put your love in writing,
  So now and then I had an inspiration ...

CHRISTIAN [*from here on, becoming increasingly suspicious*]
    I see.
CYRANO
        It's perfectly natural.
CHRISTIAN
                            But how
    Did you get through the lines?
CYRANO
                            Easy! I left before dawn.
CHRISTIAN
    Perfectly natural! And may I ask
    How often I wrote? Twice a week, three times, four?
CYRANO
    More than that.
CHRISTIAN
                    Every day?
CYRANO
                            And sometimes twice.
CHRISTIAN [*violently*]
    You had an inspiration, and it drove you
    To risk your life each day . . .
CYRANO
                        Quiet, she's coming!
    [*He retreats quickly into his tent.* ROXANE *rushes to*
    CHRISTIAN.]

Scene VIII

ROXANE *and* CHRISTIAN *downstage. Upstage,* CADETS,
coming and going. CARBON *and* DE GUICHE *are giving
orders.*

ROXANE
    Christian, at last!
CHRISTIAN [*taking her hands*]
                    Dearest, now you must tell me,

Why did you risk those dreadful roads, that journey
With soldiers, bandits, villains all around you,
To find me here?

ROXANE

It was the letters.

CHRISTIAN

What!

ROXANE

It's all your fault, you know, I took those risks.   340
You wrote them! Every day and sometimes twice.

CHRISTIAN

What! A few scraps of paper . . .

ROXANE

Don't say that!
I knew I loved you, ever since the night
You stood under my window, and your voice –
I never knew your voice could sound like that –
Opened your heart to me. Well, all this month
It's been the same. Reading your perfect letters
I've felt your love around me every day.
I couldn't stay away – even Penelope
Wouldn't have stayed at home to mind her loom   350
If Ulysses had written as you do.
Reckless as Helen,[1] she'd have flown away
And gone to find him.

CHRISTIAN

But . . .

ROXANE

I read and read them . . .
If you'd been there! Each page was like a petal
Blown from your soul. Each word was like a flame
Burning me up. Love so sincere, so strong . . .

CHRISTIAN

Sincere and strong! Can you be sure, Roxane?

ROXANE

Sure as I live.

CHRISTIAN

And now you've come . . .

ROXANE

                                     To you
My lord and master. If I knelt to you
360   You'd lift me up, and so my soul must kneel –
To tell my shame and beg for your forgiveness.
Now is the moment, since we soon may die.
    [*Pause*]
Alas, I was a foolish, shallow girl.
At first I loved you only for your beauty.

CHRISTIAN [*alarmed*]
Roxane!

ROXANE

                    Becoming wiser, I began
To recognize the beauty of your soul,
And then I loved the two in equal measure.

CHRISTIAN
And now?

ROXANE

                       Now your dear letters prove
Your soul alone is worthy of my love.

CHRISTIAN [*drawing back*]
No!

ROXANE

370   Are you happy now? A noble mind
Must suffer so to think that it is loved
For trivial reasons. What's a handsome face?
The gift of chance, which time will take away.
But thought, the power of words! Knowing your soul
I hardly see the face that won my heart.

CHRISTIAN
Roxane!

ROXANE

               You don't believe me?

CHRISTIAN

                            Please, I beg you!
I don't want that kind of love.

ROXANE

                               What kind, then?

The superficial kind that other women
Have given you before?
CHRISTIAN

                    I was happier then.
ROXANE
I can't believe it. Now is better, far.   380
This is real love, I love you for yourself,
And if you lost your looks I'd love you still.
CHRISTIAN
Don't say that!
ROXANE

                  Yes, I will. If overnight
You lost your beauty . . .
CHRISTIAN

                  What, you'd love me ugly?
ROXANE
Ugly, I swear it!
CHRISTIAN [aside]

                Oh, God help me!
ROXANE

                    There!
Now are you happy, darling?
CHRISTIAN [almost choking]

                    Yes. Excuse me
Just for a moment.
ROXANE

                Why, what is it?
CHRISTIAN

                    Nothing.
I really mustn't keep you to myself.
   [indicating the cadets]
Talk to the boys before they go to die.
ROXANE [touched] Dear Christian, always so thoughtful.
   [She goes back to the cadets who cluster around her
   respectfully.]

Scene IX

CYRANO *and* CHRISTIAN *downstage. Upstage,* ROXANE,
talking to CARBON *and* CADETS

CHRISTIAN [*outside the tent*]

                                                    Cyrano!

CYRANO [*coming out*]
    What is it? Why so pale and wan?
CHRISTIAN

390   It's over.
    She doesn't love me any more. It's you
    She loves.
CYRANO
            It can't be.
CHRISTIAN
                        Yes, it is. She says
    She loves my soul. My soul! Can you believe it?
CYRANO
    You can't have understood her.
CHRISTIAN
                                Yes I can.
    She loves your words – that's you – and you love her.
    You're mad about her.
CYRANO
                    No!
CHRISTIAN
                        Of course you are!
CYRANO
    Well yes, I am.
CHRISTIAN
                Tell her, then.
CYRANO
                            Never!
CHRISTIAN
                                Why?

CYRANO
Just look at me!
CHRISTIAN
                    She said to me she'd love me
Even if I were ugly.
CYRANO
                    She said that!
Bless her, I would have loved to hear her say it.   400
But don't you go believing it. The thought
Was beautiful, but you must keep your beauty.
She never would forgive me if you lost it.
CHRISTIAN
Why should you lose the hope of happiness
Because I'm handsome? No! It's too unfair.
CYRANO
Why should you lose a perfect wife who loves you
Just because I can string some words together
To say the things you feel?
CHRISTIAN
                          Tell her the truth.
CYRANO
Stop tempting me, it's wrong.
CHRISTIAN
                          I've had enough
Of being my own rival.
CYRANO
                    Christian, stop!   410
CHRISTIAN
Ours was a secret marriage, barely legal.
If I survive, it could be annulled.
CYRANO
Christian, I'm not listening.
CHRISTIAN
                          She has to love me
For what I really am, or not at all.
I'm going to the sentry-post to see
What's happening: talk to her and tell her

She has to choose between us.
CYRANO
                              She'll choose you.
CHRISTIAN
I hope so. [*Calling out*] Roxane!
CYRANO
                         Don't do this.
CHRISTIAN [*to* ROXANE *as she moves towards him*]
                                        Cyrano
Has something to tell you – something important.
            [*Exit* CHRISTIAN. ROXANE *turns to* CYRANO.]

Scene X

ROXANE, CYRANO, *presently joined by* LE BRET, CARBON,
CADETS, RAGUENEAU, DE GUICHE, *etc.*

ROXANE
                                        Important?
CYRANO [*desperate, to himself*]
   He's gone!
      [*To* ROXANE]
                 No, nothing, you know what he's like,
   He takes things to heart.
ROXANE
                      Perhaps he didn't believe
What I told him just now – I thought he looked doubtful.
CYRANO [*taking her hand*]
   But was it the truth?
ROXANE
                  Of course! I said I'd love him
Even if he were . . . [*Hesitates*]
CYRANO
                  Say the word.
You think you shouldn't use it in my hearing,

But don't be frightened. Even if he were ugly . . .
ROXANE [*reluctantly*]
Even if he were ugly.
　　[*Musket fire offstage.*]
　　　　　　　　　　　　　What was that?
CYRANO [*undisturbed, passionately*]
　Hideous?
ROXANE
　　　　　　Hideous.
CYRANO
　　　　　　　　　　Even disfigured?
ROXANE
　　　　　　　　　　　　　　　　Yes.
CYRANO
　Grotesque?
ROXANE
　　　　　　He'd never be grotesque to me.
CYRANO
　You'd love him just the same?
ROXANE
　　　　　　　　　　And more, perhaps.　　　　　　430
CYRANO [*to himself*]
　It *is* true! God! Is this my chance?
　　[*To her*]
　　　　　　　　　　　　Roxane . . .
　　[LE BRET *rushes on.*]
LE BRET [*sotto voce*]
　Cyrano . . .
CYRANO [*turning to him*]
　　　　　　What is it?
LE BRET
　　　　　　　　　Shh!
　　[*He whispers to* CYRANO.]
CYRANO [*in anguish*]
　　　　　　　　　　Too late!
ROXANE
　What were you saying?

CYRANO
                          Nothing.
[*More gunfire off.*]
ROXANE
                                    Are they firing?
I must see.
CYRANO
            No.
[*Upstage, enter some cadets, carrying something covered in a cloak and trying to keep it hidden from* ROXANE.]
ROXANE
                  Who are those men?
CYRANO
Don't mind them.
ROXANE
                  You were going to tell me something.
What was it?
CYRANO
                  Nothing. Just this, madam, I swear . . .
[*solemnly*]
I swear that Christian's genius and his soul
Were – [*terrified*] are the noblest . . .
ROXANE
                                    Were?
[*With a loud cry she rushes upstage, pushing everyone else away.*]
CYRANO
                                    It's over.
[ROXANE *sees* CHRISTIAN *wrapped in his cloak.*]
ROXANE
Christian! My love!
LE BRET [*to* CYRANO]
                  He was the first to fall.
[*More gunfire. Confused noise. Drum-rolls.* ROXANE *throws herself on* CHRISTIAN'*s body.*]
CARBON [*sword in hand*]
Here they come! Grab your muskets!

[*He disappears over the embankment, followed by cadets.*]

ROXANE

Christian!

CARBON'S VOICE

Hurry!

ROXANE

Christian!

CARBON'S VOICE

Muskets – raise and – fire!

[*A crash of musket fire.* RAGUENEAU *has come running up with water in a helmet.*]

CHRISTIAN [*in a faint voice*]

Roxane!

[ROXANE *tears off her kerchief and dips it in the water to wash* CHRISTIAN's *wounds. Meanwhile* CYRANO *speaks to him sotto voce.*]

CYRANO

I told her, and it's you she loves.

[CHRISTIAN *closes his eyes.*]

ROXANE

My darling!

CARBON'S VOICE

Aim – fire!

[*Musket fire again.*]

ROXANE

He's not dead, is he?

His cheek is getting cold.

CARBON'S VOICE

Time to reload!

ROXANE

Look, there's a letter in his doublet!

CYRANO [*aside*]

Mine.

CARBON'S VOICE

Aim and – fire!

[*Crash of muskets. Shouting. General noise of battle.*]

ROXANE
                    It's for me.
            [ROXANE *is kneeling by* CHRISTIAN's *body and holding
            on to* CYRANO's *hand. He tries to disengage it.*]
CYRANO
                                Roxane, they're fighting.
ROXANE
        Don't go. You were the only one who knew him
        As he really was. A poet . . .
CYRANO [*standing bare-headed*]
                                Yes, Roxane.
ROXANE [*quietly, sadly*]
        A subtle intellect, and yet so warm . . .
CYRANO
        Yes, Roxane.
ROXANE
                    So sensitive . . .
CYRANO
450   Yes, Roxane.
ROXANE
        To know him was to love him.
CYRANO [*with feeling*]
                                Yes, Roxane.
ROXANE [*throwing herself on* CHRISTIAN's *body again*]
        And now he's dead!
CYRANO [*drawing his sword, aside*]
                            And I can die today
        Happy, since in his name she weeps for me.
            [*Trumpets in the distance. Enter* DE GUICHE *over the
            embankment, dishevelled, with a head wound.*]
DE GUICHE [*at the top of his voice*]
        Do you hear the trumpets? That's the signal!
        Only hold fast, the French are on the way
        With our provisions!
ROXANE
                        Look, on his letter, blood!
        And tears!

A VOICE [*from the Spanish side*]
          Surrender!
CADETS
                    No! No! Never!
CYRANO [*to* DE GUICHE, *pointing to* ROXANE]
  Take her away, I'm going to charge.
ROXANE
                                        His blood!
  His tears!
RAGUENEAU
          Help her, she's fainting!
  [*He jumps down from the coach and goes to her.*]
DE GUICHE
                                Cadets, hold fast!
SPANISH VOICE
  Lay down your arms!
CADETS
                    Never!
CYRANO [*to* DE GUICHE]
                          My lord, you've proved   460
  Your worth today. Leave us and take her with you.
DE GUICHE
  I will, but you and yours must hold the line.
  If you can hold for even half an hour
  Victory can be ours.
CYRANO
                    We'll do our best.
  [DE GUICHE *and* RAGUENEAU *lead* ROXANE *away, semi-
  fainting.*]
  Farewell, Roxane!
  [*Confusion, shouting. Cadets are coming back over the
  embankment and falling wounded on the stage.* CYRANO
  charging up the embankment is stopped by CARBON DE
  CASTEL-JALOUX, *covered in blood.*]
CARBON
                    The line's breaking, I'm wounded.
CYRANO [*to the Gascons*]
  Come on, lads! We can hold them!

[*To* CARBON]
                                        Never fear:
I'll make them pay for two things: Christian's life
And my hopes of happiness.
    [*He helps* CARBON *down the embankment, then plants the
    standard –* ROXANE's *handkerchief – in the ground in
    mid-stage.*]
                                    Rally to her flag!
Show them your mettle, Gascons! Piper, a tune!
    [*Piper plays. Wounded men get up again. Cadets still
    coming over the embankment regroup around* CYRANO
    *and the little flag. The carriage, covered with men and
    weapons, has become a redoubt. A* CADET *appears on top
    of the embankment, moving backwards, still fighting.*]

CADET

They're coming over!
    [*He falls dead.*]

CYRANO

470   Let's give them a Gascon welcome!
    [*A huge enemy force appears on top of the embankment.
    The great standards of the Holy Roman Empire are raised.*]

CYRANO

Fire!
    [*Cadets all fire.*]

A VOICE [*from the enemy side*]
    Fire!
    [*A huge crash of enemy artillery. Many cadets fall to the
    ground.*]

A SPANISH OFFICER [*removing his hat*]
            Cé magnifique, mais cé né pas la guerre.[1]
Who are these men who seem to want to die?

CYRANO [*standing amid the hail of bullets*]
    We are the boys from Gascony,
    Captain Carbon's cadets . . .
    [*With a few surviving cadets he charges the embank-
    ment . . .*]
    We are the boys from Gascony . . .
    [. . . *and is lost in the general confusion.*]

ACT V

CYRANO'S NEWS

Fifteen years later, in 1655. The garden of the convent of the Ladies of the Cross[1] in Paris. Magnificent shade trees. The house is stage R: several doors open on to a broad terrace reached by a flight of steps. One huge tree in the middle of the stage, surrounded by a small oval clearing. Downstage L, a semi-circular stone seat set against a high box hedge. Upstage, an avenue of chestnut trees leading to the chapel, stage L; its door can just be seen through the trees. In the distance, lawns, more avenues, clumps of trees, sky. The side door of the chapel opens on to a colonnade wreathed in red creepers which leads to a point behind the box hedge, downstage L.

It is autumn. All the leaves are red or yellow except the box and yews, which make dark green patches on the scene. A pile of yellow leaves under each tree. The leaves are everywhere, half covering the steps and the benches, crunching underfoot in the walks. Between the stone seat L and the tree, a large tapestry frame with a little chair placed next to it. Half-worked tapestry, baskets with hanks of coloured wools.

Sisters are walking here and there in the garden; some novices are sitting on the stone seat around an older nun. Falling leaves.

Scene I

MOTHER MARGARET OF JESUS, SISTER CLAIRE, SISTER
MARTHA, NOVICES

SISTER MARTHA
  Please, mother, Sister Claire looked in the mirror
  Twice today.
MOTHER MARGARET
                      That's vanity, Sister Claire.
SISTER CLAIRE
  But Sister Martha picked a plum from the pudding,
  I saw her.
MOTHER MARGARET
                  That's gluttony, Sister Martha.
SISTER CLAIRE
  It was such a quick look!
SISTER MARTHA
                                Such a tiny plum!
MOTHER MARGARET [*sternly*]
  I'll mention this to Monsieur Cyrano
  This evening.
SISTER CLAIRE
                    Don't tell him, mother, please!
  He'll laugh at us!
SISTER MARTHA
                        He'll say that nuns are vain!
SISTER CLAIRE
  And greedy!
MOTHER MARGARET [*smiling*]
                    And he loves them.
SISTER CLAIRE
                                        It's ten years
10 He's been coming, isn't it, mother?
MOTHER MARGARET
  Longer than that, child. Ever since his cousin
  Fine lady though she was, chose to come back

And live her life of mourning here with us.
That's fourteen years ago.
SISTER MARTHA
                   And ever since
He's been the only one who makes her smile.
NOVICES
He *is* funny, even though he teases us –
And when he comes, we make him special cakes.
SISTER MARTHA
He's not religious, though.
SISTER CLAIRE
                But we'll convert him!
NOVICES
Of course we will!
MOTHER MARGARET
           Now, children, I forbid you
To raise the subject with him any more.   20
Leave him alone or else you'll stop him coming.
SISTER MARTHA
But God . . .
MOTHER MARGARET
         God, I imagine, knows him very well.
SISTER MARTHA
But he's so wicked! Every time he comes
He tells me, 'Sister, I ate meat yesterday.'
MOTHER MARGARET
Oh, does he? I can tell you that last Friday
He didn't eat at all.
SISTER MARTHA
           At all! Poor man!
MOTHER MARGARET
He's very poor indeed, you know.
SISTER MARTHA
               Who told you?
MOTHER MARGARET
Monsieur Le Bret, his friend.
SISTER MARTHA
             Does no one help him?

MOTHER MARGARET
  He wouldn't accept it.
    [ROXANE *appears in the chestnut walk all dressed in black,*
    walking slowly with DE GUICHE, *now elderly but still*
    magnificent.]
MOTHER MARGARET [*rising*]
                    Now we must go in.
  Madame Madeleine has a visitor.
SISTER MARTHA [*sotto voce, to* SISTER CLAIRE]
                              Who is it?
SISTER CLAIRE [*ditto*]
  I think it's the Duc de Grammont.
SISTER MARTHA
                          Really!
  He hasn't been here for months.
SISTER CLAIRE
                          He's very busy.
NOVICES
  The court ... The war ...
SISTER CLAIRE [*importantly*]
                    Worldly preoccupations ...
    [*They follow* MOTHER MARGARET *out.* ROXANE *and* DE
    GUICHE *come downstage and stop by the tapestry frame.*
    Pause.]

                          Scene II

    ROXANE, DE GUICHE (*now the* DUC DE GRAMMONT),
    later LE BRET *and* RAGUENEAU

DE GUICHE
  So you mean to live here, wasting your beauty
  For ever?
ROXANE
          For ever.

DE GUICHE
                    Guarding his memory?
ROXANE
                                                  Yes.
DE GUICHE
  Can you forgive me?
ROXANE
                              Living here, I must.
DE GUICHE
  He was unique, then?
ROXANE
                              Anyone who knew him
  Could tell you that.
DE GUICHE
                          I never had that honour.
  And you still wear his letter over your heart?
ROXANE
  Like a scapular, yes. The last he ever wrote me.   40
DE GUICHE
  Dead, you still love him.
ROXANE
                                He's not dead to me.
  I feel as if our hearts still beat together:
  I live surrounded by his living love.
DE GUICHE
  Does Cyrano still visit?
ROXANE
                              Dear old friend!
  He comes every week to bring me the news.
  Each Saturday they set a chair for him
  Under the tree there, if the weather's fine.
  I bring out my embroidery and wait.
  Then, as the clock strikes, I hear his cane
  Come tapping down the steps; he sits and laughs   50
  At my endless needlework, tells me the latest news,
  And . . .
      [*Enter* LE BRET, *at the head of the steps.*]
                  Le Bret! Tell me, how is our friend?

LE BRET
  Ill.
DE GUICHE
    I'm sorry to hear it.
ROXANE
                        Don't worry –
  Le Bret always exaggerates.
LE BRET
                        No, madam.
  All of my darkest fears are coming true.
  He's still writing his squibs against fake nobles,
  Fake piety, fake heroes – everyone!
ROXANE
  But everyone is frightened of his sword.
  No one will dare attack him.
LE BRET
                        Let us hope not!
60 It's not swordsmen I fear, but loneliness,
  Hunger and cold December winds creeping
  Into his room – those are the enemies who
  Will be the death of him. Each day he pulls
  His belt a little tighter; his poor nose
  Is the colour of old ivory, and his clothes!
  He's nothing left but one old black serge doublet.
DE GUICHE
  Not a success, then: but you shouldn't feel
  Too sorry for him.
LE BRET [with a bitter smile]
                        My lord marshal!
DE GUICHE
                        No.
  He's lived the life he wanted, always free
  In thought and deed.
LE BRET [same expression]
70   Your Grace is pleased to say so.
DE GUICHE [with dignity]
  I know that I have everything and he
  Has nothing. Still, I'd like to shake his hand.

Goodbye, sir.

[*Saluting* LE BRET, *he begins to leave.* ROXANE *moves to show him out. He follows her up the steps, but presently stops and turns.*]

                  I sometimes envy him.
There's such a thing as too complete success,
And even when one has done nothing wrong –
Not really wrong – a certain slight unease
That isn't quite remorse will come to haunt one
When rising to great office. As one climbs,
The ducal ermine trails along a wake
Of rustling dead illusions and regrets,   80
Just as these autumn leaves catch in your train.

ROXANE [*ironically*]
You're thoughtful today!

DE GUICHE
                Yes.

[*Suddenly*]

                  Monsieur Le Bret!
[*To* ROXANE] Will you excuse us?
     [*He goes to* LE BRET *and speaks quietly to him.*]

DE GUICHE
              A word about your friend.
It's true, no one would dare attack him, but
He does have enemies. Just yesterday
I heard it said, at cards, in the Queen's chamber:
'That Cyrano might have an accident'.

LE BRET
               Indeed!

DE GUICHE
Yes. So make sure that he stays at home
And tell him to be careful.

LE BRET [*despairingly*]
             Careful! Him!
He's meant to be coming here, I'll warn him.

ROXANE [*still on the steps, to a* NUN *coming towards her*]
              Yes?   90

NUN

It's Ragueneau, madam, asking if you'll see him.

ROXANE

Let him come in.
    [*To* LE BRET *and* DE GUICHE]
                    He's fallen on hard times,
Poor man. He left his shop to be an author
And he's been everything else: an actor . . .

LE BRET

Bath attendant . . .

ROXANE

                    Music master . . .

LE BRET

                                    Barber . . .

ROXANE

What will he be today, I wonder?
    [RAGUENEAU *rushes on.*]

RAGUENEAU

                                    Madam!
    [*Noticing* LE BRET]
Oh, sir!

ROXANE [*smiling*]

        Now, tell your woes to Le Bret,
I'll be back in a moment.

RAGUENEAU

                    But madam . . .
    [ROXANE *goes through the door with* DE GUICHE.
    RAGUENEAU *runs down to* LE BRET.]

Scene III

LE BRET, RAGUENEAU

RAGUENEAU

                                           Anyway,
It's better if I tell you first. I was going
To visit Cyrano, I was near his house   100
When I saw him come out. Well, he turned the corner
And I ran after him, when suddenly
As he passed under a window, a man leaned out
And dropped a log of wood on his head! Do you think
It could have been an accident?

LE BRET

                                Of course not!
A log of wood! The cowards! And did Cyrano . . .

RAGUENEAU

When I got there I saw him on the ground,
His head split open.

LE BRET

                         Have they killed him?

RAGUENEAU

                                   No.
I carried him home.

LE BRET

                       Dear God! Call that a home!
Is he in pain?

RAGUENEAU

                 No, he's unconscious. Then   110
I found him a doctor, a young friend of his.

LE BRET

We mustn't tell Roxane – what did he say,
The doctor?

RAGUENEAU

                Something about a brain fever.
Meningo-something – oh, if you had seen him!
So pale, his head all bandaged, all alone!

We must go to him now. The doctor said
If he gets up he'll die.
LE BRET
                                Quickly, this way,
Round by the chapel.
        [ROXANE *appears at the head of the steps and sees* LE BRET
        and RAGUENEAU *in the colonnade, heading for the side
        door of the chapel.*]
ROXANE
                                Monsieur Le Bret!
        [*No answer. They disappear.*]
                                                What now?
Some story of poor Ragueneau's, no doubt.

Scene IV

ROXANE, *alone, then, briefly, two* NUNS

ROXANE
120   A perfect autumn day. For a sad heart
April is hard to bear, but when September
Is fine like this, it's easier to smile.
        [*She sits at her frame. Two* NUNS *come out of the house
        carrying a large armchair.*]
You've brought his chair – my old friend's old chair!
SISTER MARTHA
But it's our best!
ROXANE
                        I'm sorry, sister – thank you.
        [*The* NUNS *retire.*]
He'll be here in a moment.
        [*She sits down. The clock strikes.*]
                                There! That's the clock.
Where is my wool? . . . That's strange, the clock has struck
And he's not here . . . he's never late! . . . I know,
The sister portress must be preaching to him

About his sins . . . she *is* preaching today . . .
Where is my thimble? . . . there it is . . . look, a leaf!   130
   [*A dead leaf has fallen on her work. She flicks it off.*]
Nothing could keep him away . . . Where are my scissors?
   [*A* NUN, *appearing at the head of the steps.*]

NUN
Monsieur de Bergerac.
ROXANE [*to herself, without looking round*]
                What did I say?

Scene V

ROXANE, CYRANO *and briefly* SISTER MARTHA

[*Enter* CYRANO, *very pale, his hat pulled down over his
eyes. The nun who brought him in retires. He begins to
walk down the steps, with difficulty, leaning on his cane.*
ROXANE *goes on with her work.*]

ROXANE
These autumn colours are so difficult . . .
   [*Turning to* CYRANO, *gently scolding*]
Why, there you are – late for the first time
In fourteen years.
CYRANO [*in a cheerful voice, contrasting with his appearance*]
             I know. Somebody held me up.

ROXANE
Who was he?
CYRANO
        She.[1]

ROXANE
           But you got rid of her.
CYRANO
Yes. I said, I'm sorry, but it's Saturday.
I've an appointment that I never miss.
Come back in an hour.
ROXANE

                        Oh, an hour won't do:
I plan to keep you here till evening.
CYRANO [*gently*]
                                        Well,
I may have to be gone a little sooner.
    [*He closes his eyes and is silent for a moment.* SISTER
    MARTHA *comes out of the chapel and crosses the stage
    towards the steps.* ROXANE *sees her and signals to her.*]
ROXANE [*to* CYRANO]
Aren't you going to tease young Sister Martha?
CYRANO [*coming to*]
Of course! Is that you, sister? Come over here.
    [*She goes to him, eyes lowered modestly.*]
Why won't you ever look me in the eye?
SISTER MARTHA [*smiling*]
Why sir, you know . . .
    [*She raises her eyes and sees his face.*]
                        Oh!
CYRANO [*sotto voce, indicating* ROXANE]
                        Shh! Not a word!
[*Loudly, boasting*] I ate a beefsteak yesterday, you know.
SISTER MARTHA
I know. [*Aside*] That's why he's so pale!
    [*To* CYRANO, *sotto voce*]
                                    After your visit,
    Sir, will you come to the refectory
    And drink some soup? Do come.
CYRANO
                            I will, I will.
SISTER MARTHA
That's the way.
ROXANE [*hearing them whispering*]
                    Are you converting him?
SISTER MARTHA
No, madam, no, he's far too bad for me!
CYRANO
Yes, but you're always full of holy gossip –
What's different today?

[*He hesitates, as if he were trying to think of a new way of
teasing her.*]
                                    Well, little sister,
I can surprise you too: you've my permission
To pray for me this evening, in the chapel.
ROXANE
This *is* new.
CYRANO [*laughing*]
                        Sister Martha's quite astonished.
SISTER MARTHA [*gently*]
I've often prayed for you – without permission.
      [*She goes back into the house.* CYRANO *turns to* ROXANE,
      looks at the tapestry.]
CYRANO
Still the same tapestry – damned if I'll see it finished.
ROXANE
You always say that.
      [*A passing breeze blows down a few leaves.*]
CYRANO
                            The leaves!
ROXANE
                                  Look at the colour –
Venetian blond.
CYRANO
                      Such a short way to fall,   160
And soon they will be rotting on the ground.
And yet they make their final flight so graceful.
ROXANE
You're melancholy.
CYRANO
                          Not at all, Roxane.
ROXANE
Let the leaves be, then, and tell me your news.
CYRANO
Last Saturday, a most presumptuous fever
Attacked the King's person – he *had* had six helpings of
   cake.

The punishment for its lèse-majesty
Was two strokes of the lancet. After bleeding
Our monarch's royal pulse regained its beat.
   [*He is very pale now and obviously struggling to continue.*
   ROXANE's *head is still bent over her work.*]

170   Sunday: the great ball in the Queen's chamber
Was lit by more than seven hundred candles
Of finest wax. The courts have burned four witches.
They say Turenne has beaten John of Austria,[2]
And Madame d'Athis' little dog was sick
And had to have an enema.

ROXANE
                  For shame!

CYRANO
Monday, nothing. Oh, no, I forgot
Dear Lygdamire has got another lover.

ROXANE
Really.

CYRANO [*growing ever weaker*]
       Tuesday, the court was at Versailles.
Madame Montglat said to Fieschi . . . no . . .

180   Mazarin's niece, our Queen to be – or nearly –
Said to Montglat . . . and on the twenty-sixth . . .
   [*His eyes close, his head drops. Silence. Not hearing his*
   voice, ROXANE *raises her head, looks at him and jumps to*
   her feet in alarm.]

ROXANE
He's fainted!
[*Rushing to him*]
         Cyrano!

CYRANO [*opening his eyes, vaguely*]
           What? Who is it?
   [*Seeing* ROXANE *bending over him, he pulls his hat down*
   further over his head and shrinks back in his chair.]

CYRANO
Don't worry, it's nothing, leave me alone.
My wound, you know – the old one, from Arras . . .

ROXANE
  Poor Cyrano!
CYRANO
                  It'll soon pass.
  [*With a huge effort, he smiles.*]
                                There, it's gone.
ROXANE
  We all have our own old wounds: mine is here
    [*Touching her heart*]
  And it still hurts: here, under his letter.
  The paper is yellowing now, but you can still
  See the tears – and the blood.
CYRANO
                                Didn't you say
  You'd let me read it one day?
ROXANE [*doubtfully*]
                                Read it? You?   190
CYRANO
  I think the time has come – if you'll allow me?
    [ROXANE, *with some reluctance, takes a little bag from
    around her neck and hands it to* CYRANO.]
ROXANE
  Take it.
CYRANO [*taking it from her*]
          May I?
ROXANE
                  Yes. Open it. Read it.
  [*She folds up her frame and puts away her wools.*]
CYRANO [*reading*]
  Goodbye, my dearest, I am going to die . . .
ROXANE [*astonished*]
  Must you read it aloud?
CYRANO
                      . . . Perhaps today.
  My heart is full of love I've never spoken,
  And now – to die. My eyes, my doting looks
  Shall never, never more . . .

ROXANE
                              You do read well.
CYRANO
  Alight like kisses on your slightest gesture –
  As when you touch your forehead – there – like that –
200 *I can see it now, and I want to cry out . . .*
ROXANE [*troubled*]
  The way you read . . .
    [*It is getting darker.*]
CYRANO
                              And I do, I do cry out
  Goodbye for ever, darling, sweetheart, treasure . . .
ROXANE
  Your voice . . .
CYRANO
                      My dearest love . . .
ROXANE [*with a start*]
                                  Your voice! I know
  I've heard that voice before!
    [*Quietly she moves towards* CYRANO, *goes behind the
    chair and leans forward to read the letter. It is quite dark
    now.*]
CYRANO
                          My heart is yours,
  Has always been and will be, now and for ever
  Loving you above all things . . .
ROXANE [*putting her hand on his shoulder*]
                                  But it's dark!
  How can you see to read?
    [CYRANO *starts, turns round, sees her so close to him,
    trembles, lowers his head. A long pause. Then, slowly,
    clasping her hands,* ROXANE *speaks.*]
ROXANE
                          For fourteen years
  You've played the old friend, come to amuse me . . .
CYRANO
  Roxane!

ROXANE
> It was you.

CYRANO
> No, Roxane, no!

ROXANE
I should have guessed when I heard him say my name.   210

CYRANO
I swear it wasn't me!

ROXANE
> I see it now.
You wrote the letters. Those wild, passionate words,
Were yours.

CYRANO
> No!

ROXANE
> The voice in the night was you.
The soul was yours!

CYRANO
> I swear I didn't love you,
He did.

ROXANE
> No, you, you loved me.

CYRANO [*his voice failing*]
> No . . .

ROXANE
You see, you're weakening.

CYRANO
> My dearest love,
I never loved you.
[*Pause.*]

ROXANE
> I feel the dead past
Is coming back to life. But why, why
Keep silence fourteen years about a letter
He didn't write – a letter with your tears on it?   220

CYRANO [*giving her back the letter*]
The tears were mine, but Christian shed the blood.

ROXANE
   Then why break silence here today?
CYRANO
                                                   Why?
   [*Enter* LE BRET *and* RAGUENEAU, *running.*]

Scene VI

CYRANO, ROXANE, LE BRET, RAGUENEAU

LE BRET
   There he is, I thought as much!
CYRANO [*smiling, drawing himself up in his chair*]
                                                   Le Bret!
LE BRET
   You're mad! He's mad! This will kill him.
ROXANE
                                                   What!
   When he fainted just now, was that . . .
CYRANO
                                           Yes, I forgot
   My last piece of news. Today, the twenty-sixth,
   Just before noon, Monsieur de Bergerac
   Was murdered.
      [*He takes off his hat, revealing his bandaged head.*]
ROXANE
                     What! God help us! Cyrano!
   What have they done to you? Why?
CYRANO
                                           Run through the heart
230   By a hero's sword, that's what I said, but look!
   Here is my real fate, struck from behind
   With a lump of wood, by a servant – even my death
   Will have been laughable.
RAGUENEAU [*in tears*]
                             Don't say that, sir.

CYRANO

    Do stop blubbing, Ragueneau, and tell me,
    What are you doing these days? Still in the theatre?

RAGUENEAU [*through his tears*]

    Snuffing the candles for Molière.

CYRANO

                      Molière!

RAGUENEAU

    Yes, but I'm leaving soon. I can't abide
    The way he steals your jokes. Just yesterday
    In *Scapin*, a whole scene was yours – you know,
    The galley scene, 'But what possessed him . . . ?'[1] stolen!   240

CYRANO

    It doesn't matter. The scene worked, didn't it?

RAGUENEAU

    Perfectly! [*sniffing*] How they laughed!

CYRANO

                    That's been my role:
    Off in the wings, feeding the lines to others . . .
      [*To* ROXANE]
    Do you remember the night when Christian courted you
    Under the balcony? All my life is there.
    I was below, hidden among the shadows
    While he climbed up to claim the kiss of triumph.
    And that was only right, I hold no grudges:
    Molière's a great man and Christian was . . .
      [*The bell sounds, and we see the nuns entering the chestnut
      walk, filing in to chapel.*]
    They're going to chapel – good. I hear the bell.   250
    The organ too – a musical accompaniment.
    I like that.

ROXANE [*rising and moving towards the nuns*]

            Sister!

CYRANO [*holding her back*]

                Don't go after them.
    When you come back I might be gone.

ROXANE

                       Don't say that!

I love you, you must live!

CYRANO
                              No. In the stories
When Beauty says 'I love you', then the Beast
Turns to a handsome prince. But in this version
The Beast is here to stay.

ROXANE [*passionately*]
                              And I'm to blame!

CYRANO
                                        No.
I'd never known affection from a woman.
My mother found it hard to look at me.
260   I never had a sister. Later on
I shrank away from women's mocking eyes.
In you at least I had a friend: for once
I heard a silken rustle in my life.
      [*The moon has appeared behind the trees.* LE BRET *points
      it out to* CYRANO.]

LE BRET
Look, here comes your other friend.

CYRANO [*smiling*]
                              I see her.
I'll join her presently – no rockets this time . . .

ROXANE [*despairingly*] I only ever loved one man, and now
I'm losing him again!

CYRANO [*to* LE BRET]
                        That's where I'm going,
The moon – no heaven for me.² They say I'll find
Good company there – Socrates, Galileo . . .

LE BRET [*furiously*]
270   How can life be so stupid, so unjust?
A mighty heart, a poet's soul, to die
Like this.

CYRANO
              Good old Le Bret, grumbling as usual.

LE BRET [*in tears*]
My dear old friend . . .

CYRANO [*sitting up suddenly, wild-eyed*]
                    The boys from Gascony!
The elemental mass . . . that is the question . . .
LE BRET
His learning still, in his delirium!
CYRANO
If we believe Copernicus . . .
ROXANE
                         God help him!
CYRANO
But what possessed him, why did the boy go
Into that galley?
       Philosopher, musician,
       Swordsman, poet, physician   280
       Master of deadly repartee,
       Lover – alas, no lover he –
       Here lies Hercule-Savinien
       De Cyrano de Bergerac
Excuse me, friends, I mustn't keep her waiting:
The moon has come to fetch me.
       [*He falls back into his chair.* ROXANE's *weeping brings
       him back to reality; he looks at her and gently caresses her
       widow's veil.*]
Never stop mourning him, that charming Christian,
So good, so beautiful; but when I'm gone
Say that you'll sometimes give your widow's weeds
A double sense, and shed a tear for me.   290
ROXANE
I will, I swear it.
       [*A great shudder runs through* CYRANO *and he suddenly
       rises to his feet.*]
CYRANO
                    No, not sitting down!
       [*The others rush to support him.*]
Don't touch me, no one touch me. Just the tree.
       [*He leans against the tree. Pause.*]

I feel her coming now: my boots are marble,
My gloves of lead . . . Well, if she's on her way
I'll meet her standing up, with sword in hand.
[*He stands as straight as he can, draws his sword.*]

LE BRET
Cyrano!

ROXANE [*almost fainting*]
      Cyrano!
[*They draw back from him, almost as if they too could see Death.*]

CYRANO
              Do you know, I think
She's looking at my nose, that noseless thing . . .
[*Adopts a fencing posture*]
What's that? It's pointless? Well, of course it is.
Whoever fought because he hoped to win?
Hopeless odds make the beauty of the thing.
Another thousand of you? Very well.
I know you all, all my old enemies.
Lies! Take that! Ha! Compromise, Spite,
Cowardice! [*Thrusts at the air*]
              Will I come to an arrangement?
No! Never! Ah, here comes Stupidity!
I knew you'd get me in the end, but still
I'll go down fighting, fighting, fighting . . .
[*He whirls his sword in great circles around his head, then stops, gasping for breath.*]
Yes, you can take it all: the poet's crown,
The lover's garland, yet there's something still
That will be always mine, and when today
I go into God's presence, there I'll doff it
And sweep the heavenly pavement with a gesture –
Something I'll take unstained out of this world
In spite of you . . .
[*The sword drops from his hands, he staggers backwards and falls into the arms of* LE BRET *and* RAGUENEAU. ROXANE *bends gently forward to kiss him on the brow.*]

ROXANE

What, dearest?

CYRANO [*recognizing her and smiling*]

My panache.

CURTAIN

Notes

ACT I

1. *the Hotel de Bourgogne*: Literally, Burgundy House. This was the more highly regarded of the two permanently established theatres in Paris in 1640. Many theatres of the day were converted indoor tennis courts, but the Hotel de Bourgogne was a purpose-built hall. Many of Corneille's, and later of Racine's tragedies were created there (though not *Le Cid*, despite the reference at I, i, 28). The resident company included tragedians like Bellerose and Montfleury, and farce specialists like Jodelet (who in the last years of his life deserted to Molière's company and appears in *Les Précieuses ridicules*). Montfleury was indeed grossly fat, but that did not stop him playing heroes and lovers until his death in 1667: Molière cruelly impersonates him in *L'Impromptu de Versailles* (1662). There is much evidence to show that theatrical performances in the 1630s and early 1640s could be rowdy affairs (see Lough, 1957), but Cyrano's public challenging of Montfleury, first mentioned in 1693, is probably apocryphal. Rostand's knowledge of seventeenth-century performance conditions seems to come largely from Samuel Chappuzeau's *Le Théâtre français* (1674), which had appeared in a modern edition in 1875.
2. *La Clorise*: In fact first staged in 1631, a pastoral drama by Balthazar Baro (1585–1650), a mediocre dramatist admired in *précieuse* circles (see Historical Note).

Scene I

1. *the Cid*: Corneille's first great success, staged as a tragicomedy in 1635, later published as a tragedy.
2. *Marquises*: These members of the minor nobility were constantly

mocked by satirists and comic dramatists, notably Molière, for
their vanity and stupidity, their effeminate dress and manners,
and particularly their inconsiderate behaviour in the theatre. The
stage marquis is invariably young and silly, and corresponds to
the fop of Restoration comedy.

Scene II

1.   *the Academy*: The *Académie française* was founded in 1635 by
     Cardinal Richelieu, to undertake the codification and 'purifi-
     cation' of the French language, and to set standards for the
     theatre. The names listed are those of now completely forgotten
     Academicians. Rostand is perhaps hinting that official repu-
     tations of his own day may be equally short-lived.
2.   *noms de plume*: Literary assumed names (literally, pen-names).
3.   *précieuses*: See Historical Note, pp. 199–201.
4.   *d'Assoucy*: Pen-name of Charles Coypeau (1605–77), satirical
     poet, friend of Cyrano and Molière. A reputed *libertin* (see His-
     torical Note).
5.   *on tick*: On credit.
6.   *A cadet*: At this period, in France, younger sons of landed families
     were placed with military units to learn soldiering. They were
     usually supervised, as here, by a captain, but units might not
     have more than a dozen cadets, and usually not more than a
     handful. A unit entirely composed of cadets, as here, was un-
     known.
7.   *Philippe de Champaigne*: A painter of sacred subjects and por-
     traitist (1602–74). His sitters, always depicted in very sober style,
     are often religious dignitaries.
8.   *Callot*: Jacques, painter and engraver (1592–1635), chiefly
     remembered for theatrical and grotesque subjects. His 'captains'
     may be mercenaries, or the swaggering captains of Italian
     comedy.
9.   *Gascon*: A native of Gascony, the south-west region of France
     which included the former kingdoms of Béarn and Navarre.
     Gascons were thought of as brave but boastful and given to
     exaggeration in both Cyrano's and Rostand's day.

Scene III

1.   *What's the colour, sir?*: A curious aspect of seventeenth-century
     French vocabulary is the development of an immense range of

terms for precise shades of colour. 'Faint-heart Spaniard' (in the original text, '*Espagnol malade*') is an allusion to the war against Spain in which France was then engaged, and which was being fought in Spain's possessions in the Low Countries.

2. *the Porte de Nesle*: The western gate of the city on the left bank of the Seine.

3. *The Cardinal's here*: Cardinal Richelieu, chief minister of King Louis XIII from 1624 to 1642. Seen (particularly in Alexandre Dumas's novels) as all-powerful and feared.

Scene IV

1. *buskin*: Platform boot worn by actors in Greek tragedy; hence, the tragic vein.

2. *your jawbone*: Samson slew his enemies with the jawbone of an ass.

3. *imposthume*: A purulent swelling or abscess.

4. *the Prologue*: In French, '*l'Orateur*'. A member of the company, often the second male lead, who had the task of speaking directly to the audience, usually at the beginning or end of the play.

5. *a protectress*: *Une épée* (a sword) is feminine in French.

6. *feathers, ribbons . . . gloves*: The dress of noblemen at this time was extremely elaborate, and wearing such adornments was not necessarily considered effeminate.

7. *D'Artagnan*: The hero, of course, of Dumas's novel *The Three Musketeers* (1844).

8. *Sic transit gloria*: Usually *sic transit gloria mundi*, thus the glory of the world passes away (Latin).

Scene V

1. *Silenus*: Roman god of drunkenness, usually portrayed as a fat old man riding on an ass.

2. *Venus . . . Diana*: Venus, the Roman goddess of love, was born from the foam of the sea, while chaste Diana, goddess of the moon and of hunting, was usually portrayed in a woodland setting.

3. *Cleopatra . . . Caesar . . . Berenice . . . Titus*: The Eastern queens Cleopatra and Berenice were loved by the Roman emperors Julius Caesar and Titus.

Scene VII

1. *Nasica*: I.e. 'sharp-nose'; the nickname of the Roman family of the Scipios.

ACT II

Scene I

1. *cesura*: The standard verse form of French tragedy is the twelve-syllable alexandrine, which according to convention is made symmetrical by a brief break after the sixth syllable. This is called the cesura.
2. *Malherbe*: François de Malherbe (1555–1628) was regarded, in his own day and afterwards, as the founder of Classicism in French poetry.
3. *Orpheus*: Legendary Greek singer who was torn to pieces by furious women.
4. *ant ... cricket*: The reference is to Aesop's fable of the ant (provident housewife) and the cicada (irresponsible singer). It is known to French people in the form of the verse fable *La Cigale et la fourmi* by Jean de La Fontaine (1621–95), which all children learn by heart at school.

Scene V

1. *Benserade ... Saint-Amant ... Chapelain*: Successful poets of the day. Isaac de Benserade (1613–91) was a favourite of the *précieuses* and wrote the book for many court ballets, whereas Marc-Antoine de Saint-Amant (1594–1661) is classed among the *libertin* poets. Jean Chapelain (1595–1674) enjoyed great official success (he was a founder member of the Academy), but was mocked by the younger generation of poets for his heavy style.

Scene VIII

1. *Pay the right publisher ... poems*: Lines (344–54) form the most obviously anachronistic passage in the whole play. The habits described (signing petitions, for example) are those of a late nineteenth- or indeed twentieth-century French intellectual rather than a seventeenth-century poet. Rostand admitted as much in an interview he gave to the review *Annales* in 1913.

Scene X

1. *Chloris, Phyllis*: Typical names of the interchangeable heroines of pastoral poetry.

ACT III

Scene I

1. *theorbo*: A stringed instrument of the lute family.
2. *Gassendi*: Pierre Gassendi, mathematician and philosopher (1592–1655). A follower of Epicurus, he introduced the atomism of the Greek philosopher to the French intellectual world. He was also interested, like Pythagoras, in the relationship between mathematics and music. One of the group later characterized as the *libertins érudits*.

Scene II

1. *Arras*: Its geographical position in the North-east has meant that Arras belonged at various times to France, Burgundy and Flanders. In 1640 it was part of the Spanish possessions in the Netherlands. Richelieu determined to take it for France and sent an army, commanded by three Marshals, to besiege it. This army was in its turn besieged by a Spanish force. After a lengthy stalemate the city was taken by the French, only to be fought over again on many occasions until it was almost destroyed by repeated bombardment in the 1914–18 war.

Scene V

1. *the Land of Love*: The reference is to the famous *Carte de Tendre*, an illustration to the most successful *précieuse* novel. See Historical Note.

Scene VII

1. *infant Hercules*. The reference is to the Greek legend of the infant Hercules strangling serpents in his cradle.
2. *Lignon's waters*: The Lignon is the river that runs through the forest which is the setting of Honoré d'Urfé's romance *L'Astrée* (1607–28), a great favourite of the *précieuses*.

3. *Voiture*: Vincent Voiture (1595–1648) was the house poet of Mme de Rambouillet's salon. See Historical Note.

Scene VIII

1. *sir Diogenes*: One of the stories told of Diogenes the Cynic (Greek philosopher of the fourth century BC, admired by the *libertins*) was that he was seen in the street in the daytime carrying a lighted lantern and staring intently into the faces of passers-by. When asked what he was doing, he said he was looking for a man (i.e. a true human being).

Scene X

1. *the happy English noble*: The supposed love-affair between Anne of Austria, wife of Louis XIII, and the Duke of Buckingham is an important element in *The Three Musketeers*.

Scene XIII

1. *turn my accent on again*: See A Note on the Translation, pp. xv–xvi.
2. *Sirius . . . The Little Bear*: These are constellations.
3. *methods of my own.* The descriptions are taken from Cyrano's own *États et Empires de la Lune*, (1657) later published as *L'Autre Monde*. See Historical Note.
4. *saltpetre*: Potassium nitrate. Used in preserving meat, and also as a constituent of gunpowder.

ACT IV

Scene III

1. *the Graves eminence*: In French, '*l'Éminence qui grise*'. A pretty desperate pun. Cardinal Richelieu's right-hand man was *le père* Joseph, a monk who was believed to have all the power of a cardinal while forgoing the red robes and retaining his grey monk's habit. He was therefore known as '*l'Éminence grise*', the grey cardinal, and the phrase has come to be used of a powerful backroom figure, a power behind the throne. '*L'Éminence* qui *grise*' would mean 'the Cardinal who gets you drunk', from *griser*, to intoxicate.

2.   *your point*: English 'point' does not fully translate French
     '*pointe*', which means (as well as the point of, e.g. a sword) a
     telling, witty saying, particularly in verse. The closing couplet of
     a seventeenth-century sonnet was usually a *pointe*. An English
     example would be, 'I could not love thee, Dear, so much/ Loved
     I not Honour more.'
3.   *Descartes*: French mathematician and philosopher (1596–1650).

Scene IV

1.   *King Henry ... panache*: Henri IV (1553–1610) has three
     famous sayings ascribed to him: one, apropos of his decision to
     change his religion to secure the throne and end the civil war,
     'Paris is worth a mass'; two, his wish that every French family
     should have a chicken in the pot on Sunday; and the third, his
     war-cry, '*Ralliez-vous à mon panache blanc*', calling his men to
     rally to the white plume on his helmet, which could be seen over
     the melee. Brave but peace- and pleasure-loving and a touch
     cynical, he is the best-loved French king. The figurative meaning
     of *panache* probably comes from the story of his white plume
     (see A Note on the Translation, pp. xvi–xvii).
2.   *gules*: The heraldic term for the colour red.

Scene VI

1.   *Baron de Pesceyrous de Colignac*: This and the following inordi-
     nately long names, indicative of the pride of recently literate
     families, were regarded as typical of the nobility (the half-starved
     nobility, Parisians would have said) of the South-west. It would
     be easy to devise similar names for Highland clan chiefs, equally
     poor and proud and equally mocked by eighteenth-century Eng-
     lishmen.

Scene VIII

1.   *Penelope ... Ulysses ... Helen*: Helen ran away from her hus-
     band, the Greek king Menelaus, with the handsome Trojan
     prince Paris, thus provoking the Trojan War. Ulysses was one of
     the Greek kings fighting the war, which lasted for ten years, and
     after the Greeks had won he lost his way at sea and wandered the
     Mediterranean for a further ten years. His travels are recounted in
     the Odyssey. For all this time his wife Penelope waited for him

at home in Ithaca. Many princes wanted to marry her, but she fended them off by saying that she would not entertain offers of remarriage until she had finished a tapestry that she was weaving. She would work on the tapestry by day and then, by night, unravel what she had done in the daytime. Roxane's 'endless tapestry' in Act V is obviously an allusion to the faithful Penelope.

Scene X

1. *Cé magnifique ... la guerre*: '*C'est magnifique, mais ce n'est pas la guerre*' (It's magnificent, but it isn't warfare) is what the French general Bosquet is supposed to have said as he watched the Light Brigade ride to its death at the battle of Balaclava (1854). I have borrowed the phrase and attempted to give it a Frenchman's idea of a Spanish accent.

ACT V

1. *the Ladies of the Cross*: Rostand has *Les Dames de la Croix*, but this order (founded in 1637 by Mère Marguerite de Jésus) was more appropriately called *Les Filles de la Croix*, the Daughters of the Cross. Widows of good family often retired to live in convents as paying guests; the families of Mme de Clèves in *La Princesse de Clèves* (1678) and Mme de Merteuil in *Les Liaisons dangereuses* (1782) expect that they will do so, though neither does.

Scene V

1. *She*: Death (*la Mort*) is feminine in French.
2. *Turenne ... John of Austria*: Turenne's decisive victory over Don John of Austria, the Spanish viceroy in the Netherlands, did not in fact take place until 1658.

Scene VI

1. *Scapin ... what possessed him*: In Molière's *Les Fourberies de Scapin* (Scapin's Tricks) (not in fact staged until 1671) Scapin, the wily servant, attempts to extract money from a miserly old father by telling him that his son is imprisoned aboard a Turkish galley and the money is needed for ransom. Instead of dealing with the problem, the father keeps on repeating '*Mais qu'allait-il*

faire dans cette galère?' (What did he think he was doing aboard the galley?) The phrase has become proverbial in French, with the meaning 'why did he get into this mess in the first place?'. The routine was indeed borrowed from Cyrano's comedy *Le Pédant joué* (The Pedant Tricked) (1654), but not until long after his death.

2. *no heaven for me*: This line definitely stamps Cyrano as a *libertin*. See Historical Note.

Historical Note

All the named characters in the cast really existed, and the minor ones, in general, correspond to the brief accounts given of them in contemporary sources. There really was a Le Bret, Cyrano's devoted friend from schooldays onwards, who published Cyrano's *États et empires de la Lune* in 1657, with a biographical preface; a pastry-cook called Ragueneau did aspire to be a poet, and having lost his business did end up as candle-man and walker-on in Molière's company. Cuigy and Brissaille were young officers, contemporaries of Cyrano in the Guards; a drunken poet called Lignière did involve Cyrano in a sword-fight against overwhelming odds, and so on. A young Baron de Neuvillette (Christophe not Christian) did marry a Madeleine Robineau (not Robin) and was killed at the siege of Arras, after which his young wife did retire to a convent (a not uncommon solution for widows of good family). The chief liberties Rostand takes with historical fact are in drawing the principal characters, Roxane and Cyrano.

ROXANE AND THE *PRÉCIEUSES*

Rostand's Roxane is an amalgamation of two different women with similar names: Madeleine Robineau, who was indeed Cyrano's cousin and married the Baron de Neuvillette, and Marie Robineau who was part of the literary world of the *précieuses* where she went by the name of Roxane.

The name of *précieuses* was given at the time to Parisian women who met in small, select circles in each other's houses to discuss literature, morals and manners. (Needless to say, at this time women could not take part in public discussions of these or any other topics; there were very few schools for girls, and they were not admitted to universities.) The first *précieuse* gatherings took place in aristocratic houses, notably that of Mme de Rambouillet, but they were soon imitated by daughters of the prosperous *bourgeoisie*, the class to which

Rostand's Roxane belongs. The most famous and successful of the middle-class *précieuses* was Mlle de Scudéry, who did publish her writings (something no aristocratic lady would have done), but under the name of her brother, Georges. The historic Roxane was a member of Mlle de Scudéry's circle, and there is a description of her in Mlle de Scudéry's hugely successful novel *Le Grand Cyrus* (1649–53) under the name of Doralise. The adoption of new names was part of *précieuse* ritual: one could see it – as contemporary satirists did – as mere affectation, or as an assertion of independence, of a new identity separate from that of daughter or wife. Whereas these women's given names were invariably those of the Virgin or of Christian saints (Marie, Madeleine, Catherine, etc.), the names they adopted were usually far-fetched and polysyllabic and had a classical colouring. 'Roxane' is unusual in that it is short and sounds Turkish rather than Greek, but the reference was no doubt to the Eastern princess wooed by Alexander the Great.

The project of the *précieuses*, in various forms and to different degrees according to the circles in which they met, was to assert the independence and intellectual abilities of women. They questioned the prevailing custom of arranged marriage and attached great importance to an idealized, asexual kind of love. Indeed, a great deal of their time seems to have been given to drawing fine distinctions between different kinds of love, and trying to establish correct principles of behaviour of men and women towards each other in (theoretically asexual) love relationships. This approach was summed up in the famous 'Carte du royaume de Tendre', a map illustrating Mlle de Scudéry's novel *Clélie* (1654–60) which shows the possible progress of a love affair in the form of three rivers flowing from their sources through different terrain to the sea. (This is the Land of Love to which the Duenna refers at III, v, 152.) The *précieuses* also aspired to reform social behaviour (from the rough, military manners of the court of Henri IV to something more befitting mixed society), and to 'refine' the French language, removing all vulgarities and developing the vocabulary of fine psychological analysis required by the kind of literature they wished to read and write.

All these aims, of course, brought them into conflict with the more old-fashioned elements of their society, with the 'good sense' of the bourgeoisie as well as the military values of male aristocrats. As a result, the 1640s and 1650s saw many satires against the *précieuses*, both in words and pictures, of which the most famous is Molière's *Les Précieuses ridicules* (1659), the story of two provincial *bourgeoises* who come to Paris, attempt to ape the new fashion and suffer comic humiliation. The two girls' names are Catherine and Madeleine (like Mme de Rambouillet and Mlle de Scudéry, but these are both very common names); their guardian addresses them familiarly as Cathos and Magdelon, but they wish to be known as Aminte and Polyxène. Most of Rostand's audience's ideas about the *précieuses* would have been derived from this play.

The *précieuse* ladies' circles attracted and accepted a small number of male participants, whether poets like Vincent Voiture (1597–1648) (see l. 1364) or scholars like Gilles Ménage (1613–92), satirized as Vadius in Molière's *Les Femmes savantes* (The Learned Ladies) (1672). Indeed, they often deferred to them as authorities, inevitably, since these men had the education, and particularly the knowledge of classical languages, that most of the women lacked. These traitors to the male cause, however, were a particular butt of the satirists, and Rostand makes Cyrano voice his contempt for them at II, viii, 341–3.

CYRANO AND THE *LIBERTINS*

Cyrano is based on a single figure, fairly well-known in his day, but extensively modified for the purposes of Rostand's play. The historical Cyrano was born in Paris (and not the South-west) in 1619. Cyrano was his family name: his Christian name was Savinien. He later added to these names the not particularly Christian forename Hercule, and the noble surname de Bergerac, after an estate his family owned near Paris. Later readers associated it with the better-known Bergerac in the Dordogne, giving rise to the myth of the Gascon Cyrano. He did, however, enlist, along with his schoolfriend Le Bret, in Carbon de Castel-Jaloux's company of Guards, most of whom were Gascons. He was severely wounded at the siege of Arras, left the army and only then became a pupil of the materialist philosopher Pierre Gassendi (1592–1665). In the 1640s he wrote a tragedy and a comedy and accounts of journeys through space to the moon and the sun which are now regarded as among the earliest works of science fiction, as well as satirical letters and squibs in verse which circulated anonymously. In 1653 his tragedy *La mort d'Agrippine* received one performance at the Hotel de Bourgogne, but caused such scandal that it was immediately taken off. In murky political circumstances, he was killed, in 1655, by a wooden beam dropped on his head from a window. His science fiction was published in an expurgated version in 1657, under the title *L'Autre Monde*, with a preface by Le Bret. He did have a large nose, referred to affectionately in writings by his friends, but there is no reason to suppose it was monstrous: certainly it does not appear so in pictures of him.

It is clear that Rostand has borrowed most of the facts of Cyrano's life for his character, but transposed them in time. The character in the play has been Gassendi's pupil, written *La mort d'Agrippine* and, presumably, his science fiction before the events of Acts I–IV, i.e. before 1640. Anyone casting the play has to decide how old to make Cyrano. As we know, the part was written for and created by an actor in his late fifties and, as one of the plum parts in the French repertoire, it is still often played by actors who are middle-aged. But it is perhaps worth remembering that the real-life Cyrano was barely twenty-one at the siege of Arras, and died at thirty-five. Also, since the character in the play is supposed to have played with Roxane as a child and she is an attractive girl of marriageable age (i.e. not much more than twenty in seventeenth-century terms, and very likely less), there is much to be said for casting, if possible, an actor who can appear not more than twenty-five. If he is middle-aged, his relationship with and feelings for the radiantly young Christian will also appear rather differently, and his self-confident tirades may come to seem tiresome rather than endearing.

The chief and decisive alteration that Rostand has made to the historical Cyrano, however, is to make him a Romantic lover. In fact, he is reported never to have been in love with any woman, though in the last years of his life he became a friend of Mère Marguerite de Jésus and of his cousin, Mme de Neuvillette, in her pious retirement. In his life of Cyrano, Le Bret says that he was always respectful though distant in his manner towards women, and in less friendly writers we find it hinted that this was because one of his many duels, or an attack of syphilis, had made him a eunuch. It was also hinted in his lifetime that he was a homosexual, but this imputation was made against the whole class of men to which he belonged, the so-called *libertins*.

Like *précieuse*, *libertin* was a term applied to people by others, rather than one they adopted themselves. But whereas '*précieuse*' at worst invited '*ridicule*', to be labelled as a *libertin* was dangerous. When Orgon in Molière's play *Le Tartuffe* (1669) tells his brother-in-law Cléante that his arguments '*[sentent] le libertinage*' (have a whiff of free-thinking about them) (I, v, 314), he adds '*vous vous attirerez quelque méchante affaire*' (you'll find yourself in trouble).

A person (nearly always a man) might be called a *libertin* by the pious of the 1660s simply because, like Cléante, he enjoyed the pleasures of life, dressed fashionably and seemed somewhat lukewarm about his religious duties. But the *libertins* of the 1630s and 1640s,

the period of our play, were far more thoroughgoing in their contempt
for conventional religion. Their philosophical roots, when they had
any, were in Epicurus, ancient materialism and atheism. Of course,
they could not publish their views openly (the poet Théophile de Viau,
usually identified as a member of this group, had been condemned to
death in 1623, had fled Paris and been burned in effigy for publishing
libertin verses). But shocked stories circulated about the appalling
heresies they voiced when in their cups and exchanged in manuscript
(cf. Molière's, *Le Misanthrope* (1665), IV, i, 1500–1504). The chief
day-to-day vices imputed to *libertins* by the pious were blasphemy,
pederasty and tobacco-smoking. But homosexual or not, all *libertins*
were united in contempt for the idealized, asexual love promoted by
the *précieuses*. *Libertin* love poetry rejects the Petrarchan conventions
and ranges between delicate lyrics in what, in England, would be called
the Cavalier vein, and detailed evocations of the physical aspect of
sexual encounters, recalling the less printable productions of the Earl
of Rochester. Recurring themes are the transience of physical attrac-
tion and of life itself, and the need to seize pleasures before they wane.
The notion of a *libertin* nurturing an undeclared passion for a *précieuse*
for fifteen years, and actually avoiding the opportunity of physical
contact with her (III, vii), is paradoxical in the extreme, and Rostand
was clearly aware of this paradox.

Rostand did not give Cyrano any of the grosser vices, which would
have alienated an audience of 1897, but many of his lines allude to
libertin beliefs and practices. He describes himself as a pupil of Gassendi in Act III, scene i, and the reference in the same scene to boy
musicians passed from one tavern friend to another does sound a little
suspect. His boasting in Act V, scene v, of breaking the Friday fast
would in fact have been very dangerous by 1655, and would have
been unlikely to meet with the indulgence shown by the nuns in the
play. This scene suggests more an anticlerical of the French 1890s
than a *libertin* of the 1650s. But Cyrano's notion that rather than
going to heaven he will go to the moon to commune with the souls of
the virtuous pagans is a characteristically *libertin* idea. However, his
readiness to die without the sacraments (in a convent!) is anachronistic:
it would have resulted in his burial in unconsecrated ground, something considered a dreadful disgrace. Listening to a snatch of organ
music in the distance was no substitute! The family of Molière, who
was also suspected of *libertinage* and was refused the sacraments on
his deathbed because of his profession of actor, went to the most
desperate lengths to secure a Christian burial for him, which in the
end was only conceded at night, in a remote part of the cemetery. The

real-life Cyrano died in bed, with the sacraments, and was properly buried, one version says in the chapel of the Daughters of the Cross.

There are many other minor changes and deliberate anachronisms in Rostand's version of the story, which were all picked out and picked over by literary historians on the first appearance of the play. Patrick Besnier gives a concise account of them in his edition of the play for Folio (1983, 1999), pp. 427–31. But we must, I think, accept Rostand's rejoinder to his critics: 'Un poète n'est inexact que lorsqu'il le veut' (A poet is inaccurate only when he wants to be). For better or worse, Cyrano de Bergerac is now Rostand's Cyrano, Gascon bravado, French dash, Romantic melancholy, Decadent provocation, enormous nose and all.